THE ADVENTURES OF RADISSON 2

BACK TO THE NEW WORLD

Martin Fournier

THE ADVENTURES OF RADISSON 2

BACK TO THE NEW WORLD

Translated by Peter McCambridge

Baraka
Books
Montréal

Originally published as *Les aventures de Radisson – 2 | Sauver les français*
© 2013 Les Éditions du Septentrion, Sillery, Québec

Translation copyright © Baraka Books

ISBN 978-1-77186-026-0pbk; 978-1-77186-027-7 epub; 978-1-77186-028-4 pdf; 978-1-77186-029-1 mobi/pocket

Cover by Folio infographie
Cover Illustration by Vincent Partel
Book design by Folio infographie

Translated by Peter McCambridge

Legal Deposit, 4th quarter, 2014
Bibliothèque et Archives nationales du Québec
Library and Archives Canada

Published by Baraka Books of Montreal.
6977, rue Lacroix
Montréal, Québec H4E 2V4
Telephone: 514 808-8504
info@barakabooks.com
www.barakabooks.com

Printed and bound in Quebec

Société
de développement
des entreprises
culturelles
Québec

Baraka Books acknowledges the generous support of its publishing program from the Société de développement des entreprises culturelles du Québec (SODEC), the Govern-ment of Quebec, tax credit for book publishing adminis-tered by SODEC, and the Canada Council for the Arts.

Canada Council
for the Arts

We acknowledge the financial support of the Government of Canada, through the National Translation Program for Book Publishing for our translation activities and through the Canada Book Fund (CBF) for our publishing activities.

Trade Distribution & Returns
Canada and the United States
Independent Publishers Group
1-800-888-4741 (IPG1);
orders@ipgbook.com

CONTENTS

PART I

AT SEA

‖‖‖

CHAPTER 1

FINDING HIS WAY

HALFWAY ACROSS THE ATLANTIC OCEAN, the *Zeelhaen*, a three-master loaded up with wood and furs, continued its progress across raging seas, en route to Amsterdam. Since leaving Manhattan, where Radisson and Father Poncet boarded, the ship had endured several days of bad weather. Father Poncet had found the going tough, unlike Radisson, who had enjoyed watching the crew at work, until the threatening storm had broken. Now he could see from the sailors' faces that things were bad.

The bo's'n, Johan Heyn, had decided his experience might be needed and replaced the helmsman. He was posted on the poop deck, the ship's highest point, from where he could see the heavy waves that had the ship surrounded. With a confident hand, he steered the *Zeelhaen* through the stormy waters. The manoeuvres he ordered to secure the ship were almost over. The sailors were scurrying back down the masts, having furled all the sails, leaving only half the mainsail and mizzen unfurled to keep on course.

The men standing watch hurried to join the rest of the crew inside, in the dark, cramped quarters where they ate, slept, and rested below deck. Radisson wasn't sure whether to follow. He wanted to stay as long as possible with the four sailors who were busy attaching the yards and fixing in place anything that might be lost overboard. Crouching in his favourite corner, his back against the quarterdeck that shielded him from the spray, he felt perfectly safe, in spite of the waves that bombarded the little *Zeelhaen*, a ship that had seemed so big to him when he boarded it in Manhattan compared to the birch-bark canoes he was used to.

The sea swelled and rolled, collapsing with a roar, then picking itself up again in one unending movement that Radisson, fascinated, never tired of watching. Sometimes ice-cold water spurted over his head and ran down his back from the poop deck. It mattered little: water was now working its way into every nook and cranny on board and everyone was drenched.

As long as grayish daylight remained, with more light coming up off the sea than down from the cloud-choked sky, Radisson feared nothing. He trusted Johan. But he dared not think what might happen once nightfall complicated matters for the bo's'n, especially if the storm picked up.

He had never seen such foul conditions.

One of the sailors finished what he was doing and ran to take shelter inside. Passing by Radisson, he shouted over at him to come too. But the young man pretended not to understand and stayed where he was, even though he now had a decent grasp of the Dutch language after twenty-one days on board. Coming out the wrong way, an officer emerged from the quarterdeck at that very moment and struggled up onto the poop deck. Holding on tightly to the railing, Radisson took a few steps forward to see what he was up to. He went over to the bo's'n and both grabbed hold of the tiller, requiring all their might against the raging sea.

Furious waves rushed at them from all sides. The ship heaved back and forth between the frothing heights where they stood and the fearsome depths that threatened to keep them for all eternity. For a time, they looked down over the dazzling sea below as it spat up thick clouds of white foam. The *Zeelhaen* plunged into the unfathomable night, as into the belly of a dragon. It was then that the miracle happened. The ship righted itself, cleaved through the light-filled crest of a wave, and fell back down again. Radisson was captivated by the performance, a dance in equal parts spectacular and unsettling.

The storm again picked up in strength.

Tons of water crashed against the ship's stern, each time shaking the stern cabin, where the captain had his lodgings. Violent shocks reverberated across the ship. Radisson could feel the danger growing, unstoppably. He was about to go inside when the captain burst onto the deck. Radisson watched him clamber up the dripping-wet ladder to the poop deck and hurl abuse at Johan, waving his arms about madly. Radisson didn't know why. The two men argued. The two helmsmen then turned the ship slightly to meet the water at an angle. This spared the captain's cabin from the brunt of the waves, although the ship started to roll more. Radisson had trouble keeping his balance.

As he was getting ready to at last go back inside, two huge waves joined forces, coming together in an enormous pyramid that towered over the *Zeelhaen*. The pyramid rose to almost the full height of the masts, rolled towards the ship, and broke over it with a terrific crash. Radisson raced for shelter, but the wave outran him, bringing him down hard against the deck. The backwash flung him against something hard. Stunned, he lost his bearings. He was suffocating in the ocean as it engulfed him. Another wave threw him against the railing, which he clung to in despair. Time seemed to take an eternity to tick by. He was going to live with the fish. At last, his face resurfaced. He breathed in, dazed and in a stupor, lying on the deck, which was now almost vertical. The *Zeelhaen* pitched terribly. The waves continued their relentless assault. The ship had been thrown off course and was liable to be swallowed up at any moment.

The *Zeelhaen* righted itself, barely managing to keep afloat. Radisson wondered what had become of the captain, the bo's'n, his assistant, and the three sailors who had remained on deck. He glimpsed a survivor clinging to the foremast. But the others were nowhere to be seen. Everything around him was wet. The sea had washed over all of it. Only a heavy yard had broken free of the mainmast and was now swinging dangerously across the deck, dangling from a piece of rope. The mainsail had been torn off. Radisson realized how lucky he was not to have been washed overboard.

The ship righted itself again. Radisson seized the opportunity to dive into the staircase to the poop deck. From up there, he could see no one, nothing but empty space swept by the wind and the spray coming up off the sea. The mizzen sail was torn. He felt miserable, all alone in the world. He had to hold on to the nearest halyard to keep his feet. The ship was starting to list again dangerously. Almost every wave threatened to lay it on its side.

Radisson at last saw the captain caught up like a rag doll between the bars of the railing on the starboard side. A strange sound reached his ears, some sort of moan apparently human in origin, mixed in with the howling of the wind and the thunderous noise of the water. He looked around. Saw nothing. Then he made out two strong arms hooked around the railing that ran along the outside of the ship. It was Johan, hanging on for dear life and shouting for help. Radisson tried to reach him, but the ship was tilted too steeply against him. As the *Zeelhaen* began to swing back like a pendulum, he took his chance and dashed across. But the deck tipped again, propelling him towards the sea. He threw himself flat on his stomach and flew head first into the railing, the only thing keeping him in the land of the living.

With his face pressed against the roaring waves, he clutched the bo's'n's arms against his chest, waiting for the *Zeelhaen* to right itself again before he moved. Now! He grabbed the man with all his might and hauled him in. Both men lay side by side on the deck, out of breath and frightened as the ship listed again. As soon as the *Zeelhaen* returned to a horizontal position, Johan stood up and pointed at the whipstaff, shouting:

"Right the ship! Quick! We have to right the ship!"

Radisson understood the Dutch command. Both men raced over to the whipstaff and pulled as hard as they could, slipping and sliding on a deck that continued to buck every which way beneath them. The heavy sailing ship had taken on too much water and resisted their efforts. The bo's'n racked his brains for a solution. He grabbed a rope attached to the mast. Radisson cut it with his eagle-head knife and gave it to him. The bo's'n tied it tightly to the whipstaff then held on to the mizzen mast to keep his balance. They pulled together until it felt as though their hands might fall off, contorting their bodies until it felt their bones might break. But the heavy *Zeelhaen* only half gave in. The storm was still working furiously to lay the ship on its side. They might go under yet.

Miraculously, two sailors suddenly appeared on the poop deck. Hope was rekindled. From where they had taken shelter at the ship's bow, they had risked their lives to cover the distance between them and the quarterdeck. The four of them managed to right the ship, stabilizing it. The helm held firm. The worst was perhaps behind them.

The bo's'n sent a sailor to get the crew pumping as hard as they could and told him to bring back men to rescue the captain.

The sailor soon reappeared with three hardy-looking men. Two of them kept a firm grip on the whipstaff while the five others went over to the captain. His rescuers hung on to the rigging, to the railing, to each other's clothes, to their own lives, never once losing sight of the raging sea. They made slow progress over to the captain, who was in such a bad way that it was pitiful to see. One man freed his head, which bounced up and down about every time the boat moved. He managed to free his arm and his shattered leg too. But could these dislocated parts still be said to belong to the body? The captain was unrecognizable. The thing inside a uniform had to be brought inside. Radisson carried the lifeless legs, holding tight to keep his footing. The group staggered down the poop deck stairs and went inside through a door that opened only after they had banged on it with increasing urgency.

Inside the *Zeelhaen*, the sea's muffled roars hammered against the hull, replacing the commotion of the waves and the howling of the wind outside. A muddle of shouts rang out. The fear was palpable. In the dark depths of the boat, five or six men were pumping furiously, trying to stop the water from filling the hold. By the feeble light of a swaying lantern, men dashed in all directions, trying to secure objects that were rolling about dangerously. Chaos reigned. Other men, wild and terrorized, stood rooted to the spot. The five sailors carrying the captain reached his cabin. Stumbling, they set him down on his bunk. The mutilated man was barely breathing. Blood ran down his whole body and stained his dark clothes red. His rescuers didn't know what to say, convinced that their captain's hours were numbered.

"Get the surgeon," Johan whispered to one of the sailors.

The bo's'n then turned to Father Poncet, who had shared the captain's cabin since Manhattan. Radisson hadn't seen him in days. The Jesuit was lying in a hammock, pale as death, struck down by a terrible seasickness that was regaining the upper hand. Poncet struggled to lift his head out of the hammock and made as if to vomit. But nothing came out of his empty stomach, only a disgusting grunt, a violent retch that left him wincing in pain. Johan Heyn grabbed his soutane and hauled him up off his back, showing him the captain:

"Bless him! He's going to die," he said to him in Dutch.

He didn't care if the Jesuit priest was Catholic and not Protestant. He was a man of God and could help the dying man cross the great divide. Too bad for the skinflint captain if he'd been too stingy to pay for a Protestant chaplain aboard, settling for a passenger who happened to be a Christian priest. The surgeon arrived and stood there, speechless. Putting such a demolished man back together again was beyond him. There was only one thing for it: Johan dragged Father Poncet out of the hammock and stood him in front of the captain, holding him up by the armpits. Again he ordered him to bless him.

The Jesuit recognized the dying man as his cabinmate.

"May God forgive us our sins, may God forgive us," he groaned in French, covering his face.

Unsatisfied, Johan shook him like a rag doll and raised his voice.

"BLESS HIM! I SAID. BLESS HIM!"

Poncet eventually understood what was expected of him and mumbled a prayer that he broke off from to be sick. He doubled up, moaning miserably. Johan looked away. The unfortunate ceremony came to an end when the Jesuit traced a cross with his fingers on the dying captain's chest, muttering a few words in Latin. Johan then handed the priest over to two sailors, who returned him to his hammock. He motioned for everyone to leave. Radisson was relieved to get out of there. The man he had grown to like among the Dutchmen who had freed both of them from the Iroquois had let him down terribly. What a pity to see him reduced to this. What a lack of dignity in the face of death.

The worst of the storm had passed. The wind had died down, although the waves were just as huge and continued to shake the *Zeelhaen*. The men, exhausted, had stopped pumping once the ship had regained close to its normal draft. It was faring rather well, and all risk of going under now appeared to be behind them. Johan took the captain's place. At first light, he ordered the staysails be raised between the two main masts. The crew was worn out. The fear had not yet left their addled minds and stiff bodies. The freezing water had flooded every-thing: clothes, trunks, hammocks, the deck, steerage, and the hold. The quartermaster who had come to help the bo's'n steer the ship had been less fortunate than his colleague: he was lost at sea. Another sailor had been lost overboard and the captain had left this world during the night. Radisson shivered with the other sailors until the galley stove was put back. The *Zeelhaen*'s yawing had carried it off along with the sand from the box it had been standing in. The crew was looking forward to nothing more than a warm meal. After a night spent in hell, eating would be like ascending the stairway to heaven. In the meantime, the heavy cold cut through them like stone.

Johan came back down at last from his long watch, exhausted. Before going back to his small cabin on the quarter-deck, he stopped by steerage, where the sailors and Radisson bunked. He sat down on a crate and stared intently at the young Frenchman. After a moment, he stood up and walked over to him without saying a word, stooped over so as not to bump his head on the deck joists. Then he lifted Radisson up by his clothes and held him tight in his arms, without saying a word. Radisson felt a lump in his throat. He was happy to have saved the life of a man whose courage and know-how he admired, happy to have helped right the *Zeelhaen*, happy to be alive.

Comforted by Johan's grateful embrace, Radisson stopped shivering. No one around them said a word. No one could find the words to express their relief or convey their gratitude towards whatever had saved their lives. Perhaps God, perhaps fate, perhaps Johan and those who had helped him.

The new captain released his bear hug. He said to Radisson in Dutch:

"Tomorrow, when I move into the captain's cabin, you can sleep in my cabin. You can also come up onto the poop deck with me. I'll teach you how to pilot a ship."

Radisson didn't catch it all, but he understood for the most part. He knew he could now go up onto the poop deck and have a cabin of his own, a privilege unheard of for a passenger with no experience. Johan left and the handful of sailors who had witnessed the scene looked at Radisson, their eyes burning with envy.

Two days after the terrible storm, the sun finally broke through the clouds. The wind died down. The sea had calmed. It was no longer so cold. The new captain granted everyone permission to go out on deck to dry off and warm themselves in the sun. Sails were shortened so that everyone could get some rest.

For the first time in over a week, Radisson saw Father Poncet on deck. He seemed to be faring better, but Radisson did his best to avoid him. He had lost confidence in this Jesuit he barely knew. He feared he had been misled by the relief they shared after escaping from the Iroquois. Now he wondered if this weakened old man really could help him, if the offer he had made Radisson was really of interest. But Poncet followed him everywhere and in such cramped surroundings Radisson couldn't keep giving him the slip for long.

The Jesuit was most impressed by the young man's promotion, considering him something of a protégé. Radisson's exploits during the storm had strengthened his intention to recruit this gem he had uncovered after the testing times spent in captivity by the Iroquois. It was as though he believed Radisson to be a reward sent down to him by God. Now that his seasickness had subsided, he wanted to close the deal he had begun with Radisson as they left Manhattan. He cornered Radisson near the bow.

"How are things, my friend? The new captain tells me you were quite the hero during the storm. Congratulations."

"Thank you, Father," Radisson replied distractedly, hoping to discourage the Jesuit with his lukewarm welcome. "I was out on deck when the wave hit us. I did what I had to do, that's all."

"God is great and merciful. Let us give Him thanks for saving our lives! Once more, you have shown great courage and exceptional ability in coming to the bo's'n's aid. You have all my admiration."

"Thank you, Father," Radisson replied, looking out to sea.

He dreamed of returning to New France. This unintended detour via Europe was complicating matters. But he doubted the Jesuit had a solution to his problem.

"Have you given my suggestion any thought?" Poncet asked, not at all put off by Radisson's standoffishness.

"What suggestion, Father? To be frank, I'm not sure I understand what you expect from me."

"Come off it, Radisson!" snapped Poncet. "Don't tell me you've already forgotten the conversation we had when we left. I told you we needed experienced voyageurs like you, strapping lads with plenty of pluck to travel with our missionaries to the nations we are trying to convert. We have goods to transport, letters to deliver, new routes to discover, valuables to protect... Your knowledge of the Iroquois would be a great asset to us! Can't you see what we're up against? You spent a year in Trois-Rivières, after all. Didn't you see everything the Jesuits had accomplished there? You know all this. Don't pretend you don't. You can help all of New France by serving the Society of Jesus."

Radisson didn't flinch. He was wary of flattery, even though he knew very well that the Iroquois were the Frenchmen's worst enemies. According to Poncet, the colony was still in crisis. Nothing had changed since the Iroquois had captured him more than two years ago.

"Perhaps you're right, Father," Radisson replied, turning to look at the priest for the first time. "But, with all due respect, I spent less than a year in Trois-Rivières and know little of the Jesuits."

"Your sister Françoise is working for us over there and she didn't tell you a thing? Our missionaries have travelled great distances and taken incalculable risks. Some have even paid for their devotion with their lives, massacred by the Wildmen you know so well. What I hope for us Jesuits, and for all the colony, is to benefit from your youth, your energy, your courage. In return, through me the Jesuits are offering you unconditional support and the chance to travel across America with our missionaries. You will want for nothing if you join us: the Jesuits are powerful, and generous to those who serve them."

Father Poncet was looking to get the better of Radisson, to force his hand. But his protégé had too often suffered because of what others had imposed on him. He balked.

"Your offer is tempting," he replied, "But why must I first travel to Paris? Why can't I go back to the colony immediately?"

"I told you. First, you must meet with the man in charge of our missions in Canada, Father Paul Le Jeune. He alone can pay to have you sent back across the ocean and accept your oath to faithfully serve our Society. You must play by our rules now, Radisson."

Radisson was beginning to realize all that Poncet's offer involved. The Jesuits would cover the full cost of his return to New France, then support him in the colony. He would also travel to Indian lands. The idea pleased him. Only, in exchange, he would have to obey the Jesuits and give up his freedom. That was less appealing.

"In Paris, I'll go find my mother," Radisson added. "Perhaps I'll stay with her and make sure she has everything she needs..."

Irked by Radisson's shameless dishonesty, Poncet spun away. How could this daring young man—a young man who had travelled extensively in New France and been through so much among the Iroquois—how could he possibly prefer to look after his old mother in Paris rather than head back out again on another adventure?

"Now listen to me," Poncet replied curtly. "Answer me this: How are you going to get from Amsterdam to Paris? How are you going to get back to New France? How are you going to support yourself?"

"I'll find a way," said Radisson, stalling for time. "I'm not afraid."

"Clearly you're not afraid," Poncet retorted. "You're afraid of nothing! But that's not the question. *This* is the question: What are you going to do with your life, Radisson? How are you going to put your God-given talents to good use? I am offering you the chance to lead the life of adventure you dream of, all while helping the Society of Jesus. What more could you wish for?"

Radisson had trouble fending off such serious questions when he had just survived a storm that had almost cost him his life. He kept quiet. But Poncet, who could feel his strength deserting him, was desperate to score points while he still had the energy.

"Let me sum it up for you," he went on. "The Society of Jesus will help you get to Paris, then return to New France. It will bring you to China, if that's what you want! We have missionaries there, too. I promise you will be housed, fed, and clothed, and you will never lack adventure. In return, all I am asking is that you help our missionaries carry out their apostolic work in New France. Is that not what you want more than anything else in the world, Radisson? To get back to New France and see the Indians again? You have often told me of the wild lands you hold in such affection, the lands you dream of one day seeing again. I am giving you the chance to live this dream. But you must decide. And I want an answer now."

Before making a decision, Radisson wanted some advice. He thought of his two absent fathers, the merchant back in France who had disappeared without a trace, and the Iroquois warrior who was probably dead by now. There was no one to help him. And the way of life that the Jesuit was trying to drag out of him made his head spin, as though his very soul had gotten seasick. The blood was still crashing around inside his heart, too much fog still enveloped his mind for him to say yes or no to Poncet. It was asking too much. The Jesuit, who felt as though he was about to collapse, was bold enough to make a final offer.

"I am even prepared," he added, "to give you the money you need to make it to Paris. There you can meet Father Le Jeune, who will be able to explain better than I all the benefits of forming a partnership with the Jesuits. If you promise me you will visit him, I will give you the money. I trust you. What do you say?"

"That is very generous of you, Father. I am flattered. But please, just give me a little time."

"Don't stretch my patience, my friend. I might change my mind. I'll give you three days to come to a decision. Not a day longer."

"Very well. I will give you my answer in three days. I promise."

Poncet then turned on his heels to head back to the captain's cabin, exhausted by the conversation. Radisson went in the opposite direction, watching an already pale sun drop off the horizon. On this brief late winter afternoon, from up on the topsails two watchmen gazed at the sky with concern. Great clouds were gathering again.

The ship pitched and rolled. Radisson had trouble falling asleep. He took his precious eagle-head knife out of its leather sheath and held it. He could see it now and again, whenever the pale light of the moon shone in through the window of the stern cabin in time with the ship's rocking. Ever since Johan had become captain, Radisson had used this cubbyhole as his own private quarters: luxurious surroundings indeed compared to the cramped, cluttered, and foul-smelling conditions of steerage, which he shared with some thirty sailors. The young man was so excited by the opportunity that he had trouble sleeping, what with the bad weather rattling him from one side of his bunk to the other and the sheer joy he felt at once again being able to admire the knife he had kept hidden when he lived in steerage, for fear of having it stolen.

A moonbeam lit up the sleek feathers, the finely drawn beak, the tiny little eye that peered back at him... The night became black as ink again.

As he held the knife tight in his hands, the memories came rushing back. He felt the same sense of well-being that washed over him the first time he held the knife among the Dutchmen of Fort Orange. He could not explain the power the knife held over him, how it guided him, leading him who knows where. An Iroquois shaman could no doubt help him understand. But it would be a long time before he could meet one. Until then, he would have to make do with the energy it gave him.

He thought of Shononses, the friend he had fought alongside for months. If the Iroquois had been right, the eagle was Radisson's spirit animal, the animal he should look to as an example. But Shononses was no shaman and Radisson had barely mentioned his strange feelings for the knife. On the other hand, Shononses had told him that the knife's handle was definitely not European in origin. That meant the power that emanated from it could not be European either. And that Radisson was going in the wrong direction as he made his way to Amsterdam.

He was now sure he wanted to return to America. And so he decided to accept Father Poncet's offer.

Dense clouds blocked out the moon completely. As Radisson put away his knife, he remembered the words of his adoptive Iroquois sister: "Your knife is too beautiful to use for killing... It will help you find your way in life..." He felt the lock of her hair that she had slipped into the sheath and recalled their passionate kisses, the hurt she had felt at not being able to be with him. He felt the pinch of tobacco he had swiped from his father Garagonké, the crumbs of cornmeal taken from his mother Katari's mortar, the arrowhead from his brother Ganaha, all carefully kept in a little pocket on the sheath... His Iroquois family came with him on all his adventures. They would be part of his flesh and blood forever. He would never forget the time he spent living among them. It was a shame he had had to leave them behind to escape with his life.

Radisson tried to slow down his thoughts. He should sleep.

The choppy sea had probably made Father Poncet sick again. There was no sign of him on deck and he hadn't answered when Radisson knocked on his door to tell him his decision. Now that the three days had passed, Radisson was sure. He would go to Paris and meet Father Le Jeune. In the meantime, he would try to find out if fur trading had started again in New France and if the war against the Iroquois was over. With a little luck, he would even find another route back to the colony.

Sometimes he thought about becoming a sailor. It was so exciting up there with Johan. From the poop deck, he looked down over all the ship and could watch the sea's every move. He could see the sails, all the manoeuvres, the hull splitting the waves. He listened to the wood groaning, the masts cracking, and the men shouting "Heave ho!" He learned a lot from Johan, who always seemed to know how to lead the *Zeelhaen* through the unending labyrinth of peaks and troughs. Radisson would love to lead his own life with such assurance.

On January 4, 1654, after fifty-seven days at sea, the *Zeelhaen* entered Amsterdam harbour. It had been a rough crossing. Gazing at the huge, bustling city that awaited them, the sailors thanked the heavens for delivering them safe and sound. Some were to be reunited with their wives and children. Others were off to get drunk and find company in one of the inns by the port. Everything was going to change for a time. Then they would again take to the sea, off to explore new horizons.

The *Zeelhaen* weaved its way between thirty-odd trading vessels anchored in the bay, heading for the long wooden wharves where its cargo would be unloaded. Johan ordered the sails be lowered and the anchor dropped. The *Zeelhaen* came to a standstill. Radisson looked on, fascinated, as rowboats weighed down with men and merchandise zipped relentlessly back and forth between the bigger boats that huddled close together. He had never seen such a busy port. Along the wharves, carts made their way between piles of goods. The place was alive with the hustle and bustle of trade.

In the distance, behind a dense forest of masts, stood Amsterdam, dominated by a dozen belltowers, some of which had giant clockfaces. Other clocks had been topped by intriguing spheres on high, pointed spires. Even Paris had been less lively in the faubourgs Radisson had been to with his father. After so many weeks spent at sea, seeing nothing but the water, the sails, and the clouds racing across the sky, Radisson was dazzled by the riches and excitement Amsterdam had to offer. He could feel the need to explore the world stirring inside him.

As soon as the *Zeelhaen*'s sails had been furled, Johan had a rowboat dropped down into the water. Two sailors rowed it over to an imposing two-storey stone building at the harbour entrance. Radisson followed them with his eyes. Johan jumped up onto the wharf and disappeared inside the building. Long minutes went by before he came back out again, accompanied by a tall man wearing a broad black hat. After chatting with him for a while, Johan came back on board to supervise the ship's unloading. The bundles of fur and the lumber had to be brought on deck quickly. The longshoremen loaded them onto rowboats and then onto the wharf. Johan forbade anyone from leaving the ship while this was going on.

A strange mix of emotions flooded over Radisson as he carried the furs. He had probably killed some of the beavers himself and bartered their skins when he was still an Iroquois, only four months earlier. He knew they were from Fort

Orange, where the Dutch had made him aware of the danger he faced living among the Iroquois. It was that trading expedition that had convinced him to flee his adoptive family, his village, and had brought him to this ship. Now he found himself on the other side of the trade, transporting the same furs he had haggled over with the Dutch.

He was dismayed to see the furs were still soaking wet and would soon rot. Nobody aboard seemed to know how to take care of them, after all the effort that had gone into hunting and preparing the animals, then bartering and transporting the furs. It enraged him to see that such a precious cargo could be ruined through sheer ignorance. This was no way to do business. There was too much at stake, it was too important. He would talk it over with Johan as soon as he had a chance. Someone would have to take the situation in hand as quickly as possible. But it wouldn't be him. He was too keen to move on.

As soon as it had been repaired and reloaded, the *Zeelhaen* was scheduled to leave for Spain. Johan wanted to meet with each man separately the next day to see who would stay on board with him. Radisson was torn. He would have liked to stay with Johan Heyn for a while longer. More than anything else, he would have liked to sail on and land in France rather than Holland. But he didn't know if that was possible. First, he would need the money Father Poncet had promised him. But the priest was still shut away in the captain's cabin.

Johan was keen to help Radisson and offered to drop him off at the mouth of the Loire. Then, he would only have to work his way up the river to Paris. It was the best route at that time of year, much better than the endless potholed and muddy roads he could take with the Jesuit, who would certainly not want to continue by sea.

From his small cabin on the quarterdeck, Radisson kept an eye on the door to the captain's cabin. If Poncet did not leave by his own means before nightfall, Johan would throw him out and at last be rid of the troublesome passenger. It was noon before the door opened. Very slowly, a hesitant, much thinner silhouette made its way into the light. Radisson was so surprised by this ghostly apparition that he wasn't entirely sure if it really was the Jesuit. But the threadbare soutane, his height, and his emaciated face left no doubt: it was indeed Poncet.

"Father!" cried Radisson, coming out of his cabin.

"Ah, it's you," wheezed the priest as he turned around. "You waited for me. Good lad. Now come on and give me a hand."

"I must speak with you, Father."

"First come into town with me. I have a rowboat waiting and have sent word to a friend. Carry this bag for me. I am so weak it is too much for me. Now let's get off this infernal ship."

"First I must speak with you, Father."

"Later, Radisson, later. The most pressing matter is to make our way to this friend's home. I need rest. Help me, please."

The rowboat took them to the wharf. Carrying the bag with one hand, Radisson helped the Jesuit along a steep, slippery stretch. Then they found a carter who agreed to take them into town. With the wharves, ships, and smells of the sea behind them, Poncet began to feel better.

The carter was wary of them, put off by the Catholic missionary's soutane, although Father Poncet barely paid any heed. He sent the carter in the direction of a large belltower set against the blue sky. On the way, Radisson took in the prosperous streets, lined by homes of brick and stone. In one of the bigger squares, he was surprised to see strange gables on top of buildings three and four storeys high. Dozens of horse-drawn carriages blocked the cobblestoned square. Nicely attired passersby seemed to be doing well for themselves. Further on, Radisson craned his neck to peer at a huge red clock in the middle of a belltower that seemed to touch the clouds. It was all so impressive. It was one o'clock in the afternoon.

Poncet ordered the carter to stop in front of an anonymous brick home. All smiles, he motioned to Radisson that they had arrived. A tall, well-built man opened the door to them. Once inside, their host clutched the sickly Poncet in his strong arms, welcoming him to his home.

"You will feel right at home here. Follow me."

The man led them into a spotless kitchen whose walls were half-covered in white tiles. He pulled up two chairs and urged them to take a seat around a large wooden table.

"You appear to be very tired indeed, my dear colleague."

"Oh, yes," Poncet replied weakly. "The crossing was terrible. Wasn't it, Radisson? The bad weather just would not let go of us. We almost sank and I was dreadfully seasick."

Radisson did not like being shown up. He hadn't found the crossing so bad, but he bit his tongue.

"You can stay here as long as it takes for you both to get back on your feet," their host assured them. "Our new Amsterdam residence will no doubt seem most comfortable to you compared to America! All that I ask is that you not wear your soutane or any other Catholic symbols. The Dutch are a tolerant people, but we do not wish to provoke. Father Jacquemin and I are most fortunate to be on a mission here. We have big plans..."

Their host broke off suddenly, noticing the missing finger on Father Poncet's right hand.

"Forgive me. I had not yet seen your injury. I imagine it was the Wildmen who inflicted it on you? Word has reached me of the torments our missionaries are going through over there. You are courageous indeed to have served in such conditions."

His head down, and with a sad look in his eye, Father Poncet looked for a moment at the mark left by his time spent as a captive among the Iroquois. Then, relieved to be safe and back on dry land again, he smiled as he raised his head.

"Save your admiration for the martyrs who sacrificed their lives over there, Father Boniface. I am not worthy of it. Look instead to my young companion. He underwent torture more severe than my own, and much more besides. And yet he does not fear these barbarians. Indeed, he has more affection for them than I do. Isn't that right, Radisson?"

"I am as glad as you are, Father, to have escaped them and to have arrived in Europe."

"Although you still want to return to New France, don't you? Don't tell me you have changed your mind?"

"No, Father. I am still set on returning to the colony."

"To serve us, like we agreed?"

Radisson hesitated. Was now the right time to tell Poncet he wanted to make his own way to Paris? He was prepared to swear that he would meet Father Le Jeune there. But for nothing in the world did he want to remain stuck in Amsterdam, travelling with a feeble old man he no longer thought much of.

"In fact, that's what I wanted to talk to you about earlier."

"Well, go ahead. I'm listening. Now's the time."

"Captain Heyn is leaving again for Spain in a few days. He says I can disembark at the mouth of the Loire. It's the best way to reach Paris quickly, he tells me. There, I will go and meet Father Le Jeune, as you offered. I promise you I will."

Poncet was disconcerted, as though he had forgotten that he himself had proposed this alternative to Radisson. Gradually, however, his face relaxed. A serene smile even made its way across his lips. He nodded silently.

"Your idea is an appealing one. Even though you will no doubt reach Paris before I do, since I cannot set off for several days yet. I understand you are in a hurry to push on at your age. If you swear on the Bible to meet with Father Le Jeune in Paris, then yes, I'll give you the money you need. Now I remember I promised you that. But swear to me, right here in front of Father Boniface and before God, who is looking down on us, that you will speak with Father Le Jeune."

"I swear!" Radisson replied, his hand stretched out in front of him as though he was swearing on the Bible. "I will go meet with him and I will tell him about my plans to serve the Jesuits, as God is my witness."

"Very well," Father Poncet agreed, looking relieved. "I will write a letter for you to hand over to him in person. As for the sums required, I'm sure Father Boniface can get the funds for you. Isn't that right, Father?"

"Absolutely! There are more bankers in Amsterdam than in all of France! They have come here to trade, attracted like our Crusaders to the Holy Land. But you should spend the night here, young man. I won't have the money until tomorrow. How does that sound?"

"Perfect," said Radisson. "The *Zeelhaen* is not yet ready to leave."

"Very well," concluded Poncet. "I believe we have made a very wise decision."

That evening Poncet penned a short message to Father Le Jeune, procurer of the missions in Canada, warmly recommending Radisson. He sealed it twice to ensure his protégé could not read it. The next day, he gave it to him along with a small leather purse containing forty silver *écu* coins. Before allowing him to leave, fearing he had been duped and might have given in too easily, he had him swear again, this time with his hand on an actual Bible. Radisson did as he was told without complaint, then, delighted to have gotten his way, hurried back to the ship.

Poncet was not so content. Tormented by doubt, he wrote a second message that day, sealing it as carefully as the first. He handed it to a messenger boy and told him to bring it to Paris at once, where he was to deliver it to Father Le Jeune in person.

From his position as helmsman on the poop deck of the *Zeelhaen*, Radisson admired the sails, puffed out in the wind. It was plain sailing. As long as the wind was behind them, it was easier to control the ship's speed and Radisson had the situation in hand. A few days of high-speed training had seen him make great strides, with Johan sparing no effort to make a sailor of him, no doubt with an eye to keeping him on board. But for naught. Life at sea wasn't enough for Radisson. The ocean was too vast, the ship too small, the days too monotonous. He had only one thought on his mind: to get back to New France and quickly, no matter how things were over there, no matter the cost. He wanted to pick up his life again where the Iroquois had put it on hold when they captured him.

He turned his sandglass over for the fourth time. His shift at the helm would be over in an hour. In the meantime, he kept heading for the French coast, which they were to reach by nightfall. Radisson felt the thrill of success: Paris was ahead of him, he had saved time, he was getting closer... It was then that Johan came up onto the poop deck early, looking concerned. Radisson looked hard at the sails, the deck, the sea, but saw nothing out of place. Things didn't look good, though.

Wanting to get a better idea of their position to the French coast, Johan called for the water to be sounded.

"Twenty-two fathoms!" shouted the sailor as he hauled the sounding line back in.

The captain was lost in thought. A sailor needed a great deal of experience to gauge the distance from the coastline, which was completely masked by the clouds. Judging by the latitude he had measured at noon, they were exactly in line with the Loire. But what was their longitude? How far were they from shore? That was another story.

"Prepare to turn around! Starboard tack!" Johan suddenly shouted.

Radisson jumped and grimaced. Johan came right over to take his place at the helm. Radisson watched, mesmerized, as the crew took their positions on deck. Sailors raced up the masts. He knew he didn't have the experience to pull off such a delicate manoeuvre, but that wasn't why he was frustrated.

"You promised I could get off at the mouth of the Loire! Why have you changed your mind?"

"Too dangerous," replied Johan. "We won't be there before nightfall. With these clouds, we won't see the coast. I don't intend to run aground just to keep you happy. I'll drop you at La Rochelle."

Dejected, Radisson watched as the ship turned around and set sail for Spain. The French coastline remained far off in the distance for two or three more days. Paris got further and further away. Radisson knew that Johan would not change his mind: the ship's safety was paramount. There was no point wasting his breath. He withdrew to his small cabin on the quarterdeck to try to come to terms with his disappointment. But, Radisson promised himself, another bend in the road would not prevent him from reaching his goal.

PART II

IN FRANCE

||||||||||||||||||||||||||||||||||||||||||||||||||||||||||||||||||||||||||||||||||||||||||||||||||||||||||||||||||||

CHAPTER 2

A LITTLE LUCK GOES A LONG WAY

THE *ZEELHAEN* had just tacked its sails. Despite the strong waves, the sailors cast a rowboat into the sea and kept it by the ship's side. Radisson quickly embraced his captain, the master he would have liked to follow a little longer, but now they were going their separate ways: one by land, one by sea. They kept the farewells to a minimum, to keep their sadness hidden away below the surface.

Radisson descended the rope ladder and jumped into the rowboat. He shouted a last goodbye to Johan and the crew, then turned his gaze to the port of La Rochelle. The entrance to the port was flanked by two high stone towers, which he could make out in the distance. The four sailors who accompanied him had a hard time rowing through the choppy water. It took them two hours to reach the town, at the far end of a large bay. The sea calmed as they approached the towers and they easily negotiated the narrow passage that led into the port. The rowboat pulled up to the stone wharf. Radisson grabbed hold of an iron rung and scaled a ladder. He was at last on French soil, back in the land where he was born. "Thank you!" he shouted down to the sailors, who headed straight back to the ship.

Radisson stood for a moment on the wharf. All he had with him were the clothes on his back, the warm but threadbare clothes the commander at Fort Orange and the Dutch sailors had given him, the purse containing forty *écus*, and the message from Father Poncet. Johan had advised him not to change his plan: the best course of action was to head to the Loire and follow the river to Paris. Radisson would have to double back to Nantes or Angers. How exactly remained to be seen.

A cold wind blew over the port. Four or five ships of considerable tonnage were anchored a short distance from the inland basin, with smaller boats shuttling back and forth between them and the wharf. La Rochelle was a place where people came to trade. So much activity surprised Radisson, even though it was nothing compared to Amsterdam. He walked past a group of people taking shelter from the wind and the cold next to the high stone houses by the water, then took the first street he saw into town.

He recognized the style of the two- and three-storey stone homes that leaned over the narrow, winding streets. He felt at home. But the passersby dashed past him, holding their woolen capes close. He seemed strange to them. He walked aimlessly, being sure to stay close to the port, the one landmark he knew. Merchants had spread out their wares beneath the stone archways he walked through: fabric, bricks, cabbages, bread, ironwork. He saw an inn or two. Perhaps he would stay there. His random course brought him back to the square by the port where an inhospitable gust whipped his face. Better to go back to one of the inns and ask for directions and perhaps find help.

Radisson chose the inn that looked the most welcoming. As soon as he stepped inside, the open fire that sighed with contentment in the fireplace beckoned him. He walked over and held his hands in front of it to warm up. The fireplace was so big there was plenty of room for him to stand by the fire. He stole a glance at the innkeeper and a group of seven or eight men who were chatting noisily around a long wooden table not far away. In the half-light at the back of the inn, a couple was eating in silence. The group did not seem to have noticed Radisson, but the innkeeper was keeping an eye on him. Radisson tried to be as discreet as possible, turning to look at the sculpted stone above the fire. An attractive ash shovel was propped against the fireplace, beside a long wrought iron poker. He felt better here.

The seven men finished their meal, but continued to drink their wine. They spoke loudly, waved their arms around, and talked all over each other. Radisson caught snatches of their conversation. Something was bothering them. Some of them were angry. But the innkeeper had grown impatient and wasn't going to let Radisson spend all day beside the fire. From behind his long wooden counter, he shouted over:

"Hey, stranger! What's your business here? Have you come to eat or to drink?"

"I'm warming myself up," Radisson replied.

"Well, warm yourself up somewhere else! I don't like strangers hanging about my inn. Are you Dutch?"

The young man's odd clothing had aroused his suspicions.

"I have come from Amsterdam, but I am French. I have money. I'd like to stay here."

The innkeeper calmed down.

"Well, then. I might have a room for you."

"I crossed the ocean on a Dutch boat. I have come from Canada."

Radisson didn't say another word. Instead, he waited for the innkeeper's reaction. Even in a busy port like this, with many travellers passing through every day, Radisson wasn't sure if the innkeeper would have heard of the colony. But he raised

his eyebrows and replied loudly, addressing the men seated at
the table along with Radisson.

"From Canada, you say?"

Two members of the group turned around right away.

"I spent three years there. Now I must go to Paris to deliver
an urgent message. Someone advised me to follow the Loire.
I'm wondering if he was right."

One of the two who had turned around at the mention of
Canada walked over to Radisson, looking wary. He was a great
strapping fellow, tall and stout. He stood a good half-head
taller than Radisson.

"So you're back from Canada?" he asked.

"Yes. My sisters live there, too. In Trois-Rivières."

He didn't want to mention that he had spent almost all his
time among the Iroquois. No Frenchman could understand
what he had been through.

"My cousin lives in Québec, and his sister, too," the hulk of
a man went on, pointing at the other man who had turned
around at talk of the colony. "Guillaume and I know Canada
well. This year, the sailors coming back tell us there's no trade
to be had because of a war with the Wildmen. They say that's
it, they won't be back again. What do you say?"

Radisson could sense a trap. The man wanted to see if he
really had come from New France.

"You mean the Iroquois? It's true they're great warriors. But
the French will win the day, that's for sure. No point letting our
heads go down. The fur trade'll pick up again after the war."

"That's not what we're hearing here. Seems as though lots
of *habitants* are thinking about coming back. Even the ones
who have been in the colony for years. Guillaume and I are
worried about our families."

"There are also Indians who are with the French. I've even
heard Iroquois talk of peace, with my own ears. I wouldn't

worry too much, if I were you. The sailors were just passing through. I spent three years there."

The heavy-set man now brushed against Radisson with his belly. His look was hard, his tone aggressive.

"Do you know his sister, Jeanne-Marie Hunault, née Pichon? Or my cousin, Toussaint Lafond? Ever heard of them?"

"No," Radisson replied, looking him square in the eye. "I don't know everyone in Québec. I live in Trois-Rivières."

"What are your sisters called?"

"Marguerite and Françoise. The eldest is married to Jean Véron dit Grandmesnil. He's an officer of the militia. Françoise is a servant for the Jesuits."

Now it was Radisson's turn to quiz them. The big man took a step back.

"Grandmesnil rings a bell. What's your name again?"

"Pierre-Esprit Radisson, like my father. I was born in Paris."

"What brought you here on a Dutch boat? Last time I checked, the Dutch had nothing to do with Canada."

"The French boats had all gone when I learned I needed to go to Paris urgently. We came through Acadia. The Dutch trade over there and are the only ones to cross the Atlantic so late in the season. They're the best sailors in the world, you know."

"And what takes you to Paris?"

"I have a message for the Jesuits. It's important, urgent even."

His story checked out. The Dutch were the best sailors; the captains in La Rochelle often took them on. And everything he said about the colony made sense. The big man decided to trust Radisson.

"Come sit with us," he said, relaxing. "Tell us what's going on over there. Not every day you meet someone who lives in Canada. I'm Jacques Laîné dit Legros."

41

All the men were carters, cartwrights, or day labourers. They worked together at a transport company. Their conversation was very animated because the man they worked for had been killed at war. Rumour had it his rival was planning to marry the widow to get his hands on all his land. If the couple did get married, that would mean less work for them: the rival had his own network of carters and merchants, even mercenaries to protect his men and his goods. What's more, hay and oats cost more than ever. They were afraid the poorhouse beckoned now that their master was dead.

With one ear on their conversation, Radisson tried his best to answer Jacques and Guillaume's questions about New France. He said as little as possible so they wouldn't catch on that he hadn't set foot there in two years. Maybe their news was more up-to-date than his. Now that he was in their good books, he wanted their help. When the time came, he turned the discussion back to his trip to Paris. Laîné tried to get the group's attention.

"Listen up!" he said. "Our friend from Canada wants to know how to get to Paris."

"Why Paris?" one of the carters asked. "You'd be better off staying here, believe me."

"I have no choice," Radisson replied. "I absolutely have to deliver this message."

"He's right," chimed in another. "It's not a good idea going to Paris at the minute. Stay here. Life is good in La Rochelle."

Radisson was keen to find out why they were trying to put him off leaving for Paris, but before he could get the question out, the innkeeper had set down an appetizing white loaf with a hunk of cheese in front of him.

"Eat up! Let me know what you think. The Dutch wouldn't know a good meal if they ran into one."

While he was at the table, the innkeeper set down another jug of wine. The carters roared with delight.

The tasty bread melted in Radisson's mouth as he devoured his food, a real feast after so many weeks spent eating biscuits as hard as rocks. The cheese delighted his taste buds, as soft and satisfying as a woman's touch. He felt like a new man. As Radisson ate, Jacques Laîné spoke up again to ask which route their visitor should take.

"And the Loire? Do you think he should follow the Loire? Is that the best way to Paris?"

"If he's willing to give it a try," one man piped up, "that's the way to go. If you're feeling brave, lad, that's the way. You don't look much of a pushover, so go for it. Find yourself a barge and get as far as you can. After that, well, you'll see for yourself..."

"No one will want to take you there by horse, at any rate," added another. "The Loire is the best route."

The men went back to their conversation, the volume rising as the level of the wine in the jug fell. Only Laîné still seemed interested in talk of Paris, shouting down to a small man at the other end of the table who hadn't yet said a word.

"Nicolas, you're off to Nantes tomorrow. Couldn't you take him with you? You'd be doing him a favour and you'd have a fine escort to put your mind at ease."

The man remained hunched up in his chair, his glass of wine in his hand, hesitant and silent. Four days earlier, he had learned he needed to go to Nantes to visit his sick mother. He was reluctant to leave because of the weather, and the money he would lose, and most of all because he considered the journey dangerous. He had plucked together all his courage to do his duty as a son and was ready to leave, but the thought of travelling in these uncertain times terrified him. He glanced quickly at Laîné, then at the young stranger, wondering if he could trust him.

"Speak up, Nicolas! You're afraid of your own shadow! Look how strong he is! You'll have nothing to fear alongside him. What do you say?"

Radisson put on his broadest smile to win the carter over.

"What if he's a thief?" Nicolas countered. "We don't even know where he's come from. Look at how he's dressed! I don't trust him."

"He's from Canada, Nicolas. I'm sure he's telling the truth. I've already heard tell of Grandmesnil. You'll both be doing each other a favour. Come on, Nicolas, one good turn..."

"My mother still lives in Paris," added Radisson, sticking out his chest to look as brave and strong as he could manage, but not too much so as not to frighten the man they claimed was afraid of his own shadow. "I was born there. I'm a Frenchman, just like you! The Dutch gave me these old clothes so I wouldn't get cold on the crossing. If the Jesuits trust me to deliver one of their messages, you have nothing to fear, I swear!"

Radisson went as far as crossing himself to show he was a good Christian. But Nicolas still wasn't sure. The stranger was strong and everyone said you needed to be fearless to go to Canada. He would be safe with him. He could even ask for a little money, if he worked up the courage.

Jacques Laîné lost interest with the carter still to reply. It was none of his business, after all. Neither Guillaume nor anyone else wanted to get involved. Radisson made one last effort, flashing Nicolas his winning smile... At last, the carter made up his mind.

"If you dress like a Frenchman, I'll bring you!" he exclaimed, setting down his wine with a bang on the table.

"With pleasure!" Radisson agreed. "I'll find myself something to wear tonight. Thank you!"

"Promise you'll defend us if we run into thieves along the way."

"I promise!"

"We'll meet here tomorrow in front of the inn, when the cock crows."

"I'll be there!"

That evening, the innkeeper sent for a secondhand clothes dealer so that Radisson could buy the French clothes he needed. He kept only the old wool sailor's jacket to keep him warm. He spent the night in front of the fire, on a straw mattress on the floor, to be sure he wouldn't miss the appointment the next morning.

At the first light of day, Nicolas Petit arrived as agreed. Together, they set out for Nantes.

The cart trundled along the ill-kept, narrow country roads. Nicolas went easy on his horse. He didn't want to tire it out or break the cart. They passed by fallow land, cut through tiny hamlets where no more than a few dozen people lived, and through two small villages, too. From time to time, they met other ramshackle carts, advancing just as slowly as their own. Almost no one was working in the fields in the off-season, save for a handful of farmers spreading manure. The ploughed land gave the landscape a sombre hue. Trees were few and far between. No greenery, not a trace of snow. Radisson swallowed his impatience and the temptation to complain about the slow going. To pass the time, he told Nicolas about the Canadian winters.

"The snow is *this* high," he said, holding his arm up to his face. "Everywhere. It looks a lot better than here."

Nicolas pulled a face, skeptical.

"Don't believe me? You ever seen snow?"

"Of course! We can't take the carts out when it snows. It's slippery, white, and wet. But it melts in no time."

"Not in Canada," came Radisson's reply. "Over there, it's so cold the snow lies for six months, piling up day after day. It's cold enough to crack rocks in two—snap!—just like that! Luckily, there are forests everywhere, and there's plenty of firewood or else we'd all die of cold."

"Life doesn't seem easy in Canada."

"You need to be made of the right stuff, that's all. But there are advantages. The snow is beautiful and the cold makes you really feel alive. Canada is another world. Over there, everyone has a wood floor at home, not just the rich. You need one to keep warm. And underneath the floor, people keep their vegetables in wooden crates in winter so they don't freeze. You go down and get them through a trap door in the floor."

Radisson had piqued Nicolas' curiosity. His companion felt as though he was travelling much further than Nantes.

"And if the snow is so deep," he asked, "how do people get around by cart?"

"We slide across the snow on sleds, just like the Indians. The worst snowstorm I ever saw was like the flood in the Bible, only with snow! We were sheltered in my sister's house, but when it was over we could hardly get outside there was so much snow. The door was blocked!"

"I don't believe you!" Nicolas protested.

"I swear! To get about, you have to put on huge snowshoes otherwise you're up to your neck in the stuff! Snowshoes are like wicker baskets, only long and flat. With a pair of them on your feet, you can walk about no problem and pull the sleds I was telling you about. It's not easy at first, but you get used to it in no time. Without snowshoes, you can get buried alive in the snow."

"So you don't have any carts?"

"In summer, yes, but not in winter. For heavy loads like firewood, we hitch up a big sled behind one or two oxen. We don't have horses over there."

46

"No horses!"

"Not yet."

"Unbelievable!"

"The Indians showed us how. They've been living like that for a long time. They've got the knack of it. But it's not an easy country. Everything is still to be done."

"Then why do we keep hearing here that Canada's finished?"

"Because of the war. There are Indians who are friends with the French, but others are their sworn enemies."

"It's the same here. Damned war. Everything is every which way because of it."

Nicolas stopped well before dusk. At that rate, Radisson was sure they would never get there. When he said as much to Nicolas, the carter took a while to answer, then said he wanted to play things safe: there were bandits who attacked travellers at nightfall.

"But you have nothing to steal," exclaimed Radisson. "Your cart is empty!"

"It's costing me enough money as it is going home to see my mother. Don't think for a minute I'm going to go and have my stock stolen as well. I don't like taking risks."

"Your brother-in-law the innkeeper would surely have bought something from you, I don't know, some flour or wine. It would have paid for your trip. You didn't think of that?"

"I have a big ham with me to give to him in return for a place to stay. That's plenty."

Radisson bit his tongue, not wanting to further criticize Nicolas, who was after all helping him. But he couldn't believe a carter hadn't thought to do a bit of business. What a wasted opportunity this empty cart was!

The next morning, after they had been on the road for an hour, they came across a small group of soldiers.

"Look out!" warned Nicolas. "Take no notice of them."

As they reached the soldiers, Nicolas kept his head down, fiddling nervously with his harness, while Radisson greeted them enthusiastically. Once the soldiers were behind them, Nicolas whined:

"I told you to be careful!"

"There's nothing to be afraid of," replied Radisson, amazed at the fear that paralyzed his companion. "They don't bite."

"It just goes to show you don't know them! They have muskets and, believe me, they know how to use them. Soldiers are dangerous. They're behind a lot of the crime."

"I know how to use a musket too," boasted Radisson. "I'll have you know I'm the best shot in Trois-Rivières! Over there, everyone has a musket and knows how to shoot. They have no choice. We'd die of hunger otherwise: we need to hunt our food. And we have to defend ourselves from the Indians. It's part of life there!"

"I don't believe you."

"It is! In Canada, every day we eat the meat God gives us: moose, bear, deer, beaver, goose... Pigs we rear and keep for winter reserves. Plus there's all the fish to be had from the rivers and lakes! Canada is no country for fearful men, but it's a great place to live for anyone with guts!"

Nicolas didn't dare answer. He felt judged, but what could he do? It was true he had always been lacking in courage. But he was shocked to learn that in Canada people ate like kings; he had always thought of New France as a place of poverty and woe. Unless Radisson was flat out lying to him. He felt a little frustrated at the thought that everyone there enjoyed rights that were reserved for lords, princes, and the wealthy in France. How come there was more to eat in this colony in the middle of nowhere than the French had when they worked every waking hour for some black bread and a piece of meat every other week? It wasn't fair.

"Long ways, long lies," he protested feebly, trying to defend himself.

"You don't believe me?" replied Radisson.

"It all seems too good to be true."

"And I haven't even mentioned the best thing of all."

Radisson thought of the magnificent lands he had crossed with the Iroquois, of the boundless freedom he had enjoyed. Just thinking of it still made him giddy.

"You see, Nicolas, you're used to sleeping in inns. But in Canada, if you want to move around, you have to sleep outside, under the stars when the weather is good, or in the rain with the wild animals. Forests stretch as far as the eye can see. Even after days and days of travelling, you're still in the forest. The rivers are huge, and the St. Lawrence is as wide as the sea. You've never seen the like of it, I'm sure, because there's nothing like it in France. Canada is a land like no other. I can't wait to go back."

Just talking about these wide open spaces sent shivers down Radisson's spine. Down Nicolas Petit's, too, but for different reasons. The very idea of getting lost in a vast forest he would never find his way out of had him shaking from head to foot. Because dark and mysterious forests were what he feared most in the world. The longer he listened to Radisson talk about Canada, the more disheartened he felt. The colony was barely inhabited, under threat from the Indians, and he was sure that he would never, ever set foot there. But at the same time, it fascinated him and he envied Radisson for feeling so at home there. He listened with the same interest he reserved for a preacher describing heaven and hell to him. He never tired of it. Even though he wasn't entirely sure Radisson was telling him the whole truth, he had never travelled in such entertaining company. The long journey was passing by in a flash.

Radisson, on the other hand, was fast running out of patience when Nicolas stopped a second time in the midafternoon, fearing they wouldn't make the next inn before nightfall. So as not to lose his temper with his amiable companion, he went for a walk in the deserted fields surrounding the village.

The next day, Radisson was less talkative, afraid he might reveal he had lived among the Iroquois for so long. The news might work against him, he thought. The secret was a weight on his shoulders and kept him on the alert. He made do with telling another tale or two about his life in Trois-Rivières. The journey seemed to be dragging on forever.

In the late afternoon, Nicolas stopped his cart in front of five thatched farmhouses, huddled cheek by jowl, their chimneys smoking. Behind them, a few animals grazed in a field dotted with shrivelled tree stumps. No one in sight. The hamlet was at the intersection of two quiet roads.

"We're going to sleep there," said Nicolas, pointing at the biggest house.

"Not this again!" exclaimed Radisson, unable to contain his disappointment. "Listen, Nicolas, we have plenty of time to make it until the next village at least. Look, you can see the church steeple over there in the distance."

"No way," declared Nicolas.

They would have to cut through one of the area's rare woods and the thought of being stuck there at dusk, perhaps even after night had fallen, made his blood run cold.

"Buddy's tired."

"Tired? Come on, Nicolas. Your horse is fine! He's used to working much harder than this! Come on, let's go. We've wasted enough time as it is."

But there was no way Nicolas was venturing into a forest so late in the day. This gave him the resolve he needed to stand up to his impetuous companion.

"No!" he repeated, firmly.

"Even Buddy wants to go on, I'm sure," Radisson insisted. "Please, Nicolas, we have lots of time to make it to the next village."

Nicolas didn't give an inch, already imagining the bandits and werewolves lying in wait for them, ready to drag them from their chosen paths to a life of eternal suffering. The homes, villages, and church steeples they could see here and there in the distance didn't change a thing. To Nicolas, the forest might as well have been the end of the world. There was no way he was going to set foot in it. Radisson paid no heed to his guide's reluctance and cried out:

"Giddy up, Buddy! Come on!"

The horse broke into such a gallop that both men were thrown back in their seats, almost sending the cart into a ditch. It took Nicolas a second or two to catch hold of the reins and regain control of his horse, which finally came to a halt a hundred metres or so down the road. The carter had turned bright red with anger. He was so scared he could hardly breathe. He couldn't speak. Radisson, also surprised at Buddy's reaction, had been frightened the cart would break. But, as it turned out, they were none the worse for wear.

"See? Your horse can't be that tired. Come on, Nicolas, let's press on. We're almost there."

The carter didn't move a muscle. The incident had left him so shaken up that his whole body was trembling. Radisson wondered what he should do.

"We can't cut through the woods at this hour," Nicolas finally stammered. "We'll be set upon by bandits."

"So that's it!" Radisson said to himself. For him, the woods held no danger. He just had to find a way to make Nicolas feel safe. After thinking for a moment, an idea came to mind. He jumped up, brandishing his eagle-head knife and shouting:

"Bandits? Bring them on!"

Nicolas jumped up with fright, exclaiming:

"Please! Please, don't kill me! Have mercy!"

Radisson was bewildered.

"For heaven's sake, Nicolas," he reassured him, "I just wanted to show you I know how to defend myself. This is a powerful knife. It will have the better of anyone."

Nicolas calmed down, but still couldn't bring himself to move on.

"And what if twenty of them attack us," he asked. "What will you do then?"

"Twenty bandits! He has some imagination," thought Radisson, sitting back down. He had never met such a coward. But an image suddenly had him trembling: his torture. He thought back to the day he left Trois-Rivières, laughing at those who had warned him of the danger. Realizing he would have trouble fending off an attack from a group of thieves with just his knife, he thought better of it.

"You're right, Nicolas. We'll keep going to the next village since we have plenty of time, but we won't go unprepared. We'll play it safe."

Nicolas was just as terrified by this option, but now that he knew his companion was armed, he wasn't going to contradict him. He could do whatever he wanted to him.

"Before we go into the woods," Radisson explained to him, "give Buddy something to eat. Give him a few oats to get him worked up. While you're doing that, I'll go find us two big sticks. There are bound to be some on the edge of the forest. After that, we'll gather rocks to bring with us in the cart. That way, if anyone tries to block our path, they'll soon know who they're dealing with. And if one of them is brave enough to attack us, I'll get him with my knife! The main thing, Nicolas, will be to get Buddy going at a good trot. We'll cross the wood at top speed so that no one can lay a hand on us. Right, let's get going!"

Even though fear was still tying the carter's stomach in knots, Nicolas chose the lesser of two evils. The risk of stumbling upon bandits seemed less awful to him than having to stand up to the man telling him what to do. As he fed his horse, he prayed to God, asking him to forgive him his sins and not to keep him in purgatory for longer than a hundred years or two since he had never committed any mortal sins and was sorry for the others. Radisson found a long bough, which he cut into two clubs of equal length. He kept the heavier one for himself. He then gathered thirty or so rocks the size of a man's fist and set them down on the cart. They were ready. The carter, fuming silently, moved his horse forward to the edge of the woods.

"As soon as we're in the trees," Radisson ordered, "break him into a trot. But not too quickly. He'll have to keep going until we reach the other side. I'll lie down in the back and hide. If thieves block our path, I'll jump up. You get Buddy into a gallop, then charge them. We'll be able to surprise them. They won't know what hit them, Nicolas. Sound like a plan? You with me? Let's go!"

"This is all we needed," Nicolas grumbled to himself. Here he was all alone, having to confront all the dangers in the world at once. It was the worst day of his life. The shadows and the damp made his blood run cold as they entered the forest. But he followed Radisson's orders. He snapped the reins and Buddy broke into a trot as Nicolas stared blankly ahead and prayed with all his heart that no harm would come to them.

Radisson scanned the woods and the path ahead, peering over Nicolas' shoulder and paying close attention to the slightest sound, like an Iroquois on the warpath. He was positive he would be able to hear bandits talking to each other above the creaking of the wheels and the clip-clop of the hoofs on the path. He clutched his eagle-head knife in one hand, his club in the other. The stones he had gathered rolled about on the floor of the cart. He feared nothing. He had thought of everything.

"Keep at it, Nicolas. We're going well. We're going to make it."

The spirit of the eagle was watching over him and inspiring him to do the right thing, of that he was sure. Woe betide anyone who crossed their path. He would make mincemeat out of them. The cart moved forward at a right old clip, with barely a bump or a jolt across the even surface. Radisson was thrilled: at last they were moving forward as fast as he had hoped.

"Don't worry, Nicolas. We're almost there."

Encouraged, the carter gave Buddy a slap with the reins. He could see the light at the end of the forest. Just five hundred metres more. He was going to make it… God have mercy on our souls, he repeated under his breath.

They came out into the open. The sun was disappearing on the horizon, behind the enormous steeple whose silhouette stood out against the fiery sky. It was still light as they entered the village. The inn welcomed them with open arms.

Nicolas brushed Buddy again and again by the light of a lantern in the stables. His horse had kept trotting right to the end. He had gotten very warm, but he didn't look exhausted. The carter was extraordinarily proud of his workmate. For years they had shared everything, good times and bad. They were in it together, almost like man and wife. Radisson hovered close by them since something approaching a state of grace was emanating from Nicolas, visibly surprised and pleased at what he had accomplished. After having seen him so terrorized, it was heartwarming to see him looking so glad.

"That's some horse you have there, Nicolas," Radisson told him, giving Buddy a pat.

"Don't know a better one."

As they shared a meal in the inn, Nicolas tried to sort out his thoughts. Although extremely tired, he felt more gratitude than resentment toward Radisson, who had shown him he was more resourceful than he had ever imagined. This small victory—a considerable one, to him—had given him a taste of freedom and excitement. With a little help from the wine, he felt like he was walking on air.

Radisson preferred to stay clear of wine. The sight of his brother Ganaha becoming the shadow of himself under the effects of alcohol had left a bad taste in his mouth. He considered it more sensible to keep his wits about him. Paris was still a long way away.

When they arrived in Nantes, Nicolas' brother-in-law put them up for the night. The innkeeper grimaced without a word of explanation when he heard Radisson was headed to Paris. Radisson, who was in a hurry to get back on the road, was not worried in the slightest. Early the next morning, Nicolas brought him down to the port and showed him where to find the boatmen who were heading upriver.

Along the quay, a number of lifeless craft were waiting for spring to arrive. A few small fishing boats moved across the estuary. Only a handful of flat-bottomed boats, designed for navigating the Loire, were loaded up with goods and ready to cast off to the towns and villages inland. Since Radisson saw no captain or crew, he had no idea if he would be allowed to board.

In the distance, a stout man was having trouble rolling a heavy barrel up an incline. He caught Radisson's eye and Radisson moved closer to get a better look. The man was quite old and swearing like a sailor. Seeing him arrive out of breath at the wharf's edge, giving the barrel one last shove to stack it next to a dozen more, then sitting down for a quick rest, swearing all the while, Radisson thought to himself that the man was surely in need of a helping hand. A dozen more barrels were waiting in the barge.

"Hello there!" Radisson shouted. "I can unload them for you, if you'd like!"

"Leave me alone! I can manage. Young good-for-nothings like you aren't in short supply round here."

"My father is a merchant, sir. I've carried thousands of barrels before! I'm not afraid of a good day's work."

"Are ye deaf?" the man exclaimed, with a threatening stare. "I told ye to leave me alone!"

"If you're going back upriver, I can help. I can do anything: carry things around, sail, fish. I'd like to help you, sir, if you're going towards Paris."

The boatman took a moment to look the bold young man up and down. The morning was a fresh one, but he was covered in sweat. He spat on the ground, then asked:

"Know how to pilot a boat, do you?"

"Yes. I've crossed the ocean, sir. I took the helm of a store ship from Amsterdam to La Rochelle. I'm a good sailor."

The boatman inspected Radisson. So he wanted to come aboard, did he? He seemed to be made of the right stuff. He looked strong and honest.

"Show me what you can do, lad. Hop down onto the barge, take a barrel, and bring it back up here. But be careful! It's good Vouvray wine I have in there. Break a barrel and I'll break every bone in yer body! Now get to it!"

Radisson ran down the slope, jumped onto the barge, tipped a barrel onto its side, rolled it along the gangway that came up from the barge, then pushed it quickly up the slope. With the boatman keeping a close eye on him, once on the wharf, he gave the barrel a shove just like the older man had done and put it beside the others. A nice, quick job. It reminded him of the days he had spent moving goods around with his father: brandy, boards, sacks of grain, scrap metal... anything that could be bought and sold in the neighbourhood.

"I see you were telling no lies," the boatman told him, satisfied. "Follow me."

They walked down together to the barge, where the big man gave him his orders.

"Bring in the sheet."

Radisson found the right rope and yanked on it.

"Where's the halyard?"

Radisson pointed to the rope used to hoist the sail.

"Turn to the port side."

Radisson pushed the tiller to the right to turn the boat left, all the while keeping an eye on the top of the mast as though he were looking at the sails.

"I could always take you on for a trial," the man concluded, relieved to have found a helping hand. "So long as you bring all these barrels up to the wharf and you help me load the salt I have to bring to Orléans. But I'll tell you one thing, lad. I'll be keeping a very close eye on you. Any problems and you're off my boat. I'm not in the habit of trusting strangers, but I'm in a bit of a fix. And don't think you'll be getting paid for any of this! I'll feed you, that's all. Count yourself lucky I'm bringing you with me."

||||||||||||||||||||||||||||||||||||||||||||||||||||||||||||||||||||||||||||||||||||||||||||||||||||||

CHAPTER 3

THIS WAY TO PARIS!

J OACHIN TOUCHET knew the river like the back of his hand. He had been shipping goods between Nantes and Orléans for as long as he could remember, on an old barge he called *La Louve*. She had just one square sail to catch the wind from the aft or side, but never a headwind. When the wind was against them, he had to drop anchor and wait, which always put him in a foul temper. For that reason, he pushed on as fast as he could every time the wind was favourable. Radisson was happy to travel with someone as impatient as he was. He admired his experience. But he did not appreciate his foul temper.

After four days on the river, they came within sight of Saumur, a prosperous, pretty village. They had to lower the mast to squeeze under a fine stone bridge on the way into town. A strong current working against them made it a delicate operation. As soon as the sail and mast were lowered, the barge would slow down a little, but there was no time to lose: otherwise the boat threatened to slide off in the opposite direction and right into the bridge. Radisson carefully prepared the manoeuvre. If he didn't manage it first go, Touchet would surely shower him with abuse, as was his wont.

"Lower the sail!" Touchet roared at him. "Lower the mast! Quick!"

Radisson lowered the sail in a flash and kept the mast under control as it fell. They slowed to a crawl and crept in under the bridge's central arch. They were almost through when the boat stopped moving forward and began to drift dangerously toward the nearest pillar. But Touchet skilfully corrected their course and narrowly managed to free the back of the boat.

"RAISE THE SAIL!" he screamed. "Quick!"

Radisson pulled on the mast and mainsail halyards with all his might. The captain caught a little wind, while Radisson deftly improved the sail's angle of approach. For a long time the boat was balanced between the wind and the current, right up against the sharp, threatening pillars. At last, thanks to their combined efforts, *La Louve* started moving forward again. Radisson was pleased at himself for managing to pull off such a tricky manoeuvre, but Touchet blasted him with all the names under the sun.

"YOU DIMWIT! When I tell you to get a move on, you get a move on, you hear! I don't know why I don't just throw you overboard."

Radisson bit his tongue. He had come to understand that the sailor he was replacing had left Touchet in the lurch because there was no putting up with the man. He would be only too happy to walk out on him too, but he would rather endure him and make it to Orléans more quickly. At any rate, his anger came and went like a storm: it was intense, but over in a flash. Radisson went back to his usual position up at the front of the boat to watch the channel and the sandbanks while Touchet steered. Peace had been restored. Radisson took in the scenery of the Loire around him. He loved the river, lined with huge fallow fields, thriving villages, and impressive buildings.

Ahead of him, in the bright light of a day drawing to a close, a large castle caught his eye in the distance. Not only was its size impressive, it was incredibly elegant, too. Standing atop a hill, with its four high, square towers and breathtakingly high walls, the fortress dominated the whole region. Building a solid, impressive building like that had been no mean feat. Down below, the homes of Saumur formed a tight patchwork of red and black and sandstone and slate all around. Four or five impressive belltowers rose up from behind the homes like arrows moving skyward. The setting was superb.

Radisson enjoyed watching the wharves bustle with activity despite the late hour. Workers rounded barrels up into high piles near a ramp that plunged down into the water. A small craft drew up to bring them aboard and on to other village folk in need of them. Trade could be so useful.

The sun had set, but Touchet wanted to press on, keen to put off the hour when they would drop anchor in a quiet dock beside the river and spend the night there. Radisson had no complaints. But from where he was, he could no longer see how deep the water was. He couldn't see a thing. As he admired the shapes the town and castle made out against the coloured sky, behind them an invisible hand tugged on the barge. The sail was swollen with the wind, but they were making no headway. They must have run aground on a sandbank Radisson hadn't seen coming.

"THAT'S IT!" Touchet cried, leaving the helm to scoop something up.

Radisson watched as he dashed toward him, his back to the light, thinking he was coming over to see what was going on. But when he reached him, Touchet hit him hard with a stick.

"Take that, you incompetent oaf!"

The pain was so sharp it almost paralyzed Radisson's left arm. He managed to sidestep a second blow.

"Run my barge aground, will you? I'll teach you, you little swine! Take that! And that!"

Radisson straightened up, grabbed Touchet by the arm and used the boatman's momentum to fling him onto the deck. He immobilized him, bringing his full weight down onto him as he grabbed him by the throat with one hand and drew his knife with the other. Touchet struggled to break free. Radisson thrust the tip of the knife against his fat cheek and spat furiously into his ear:

"One more move and I'll cut your face!"

Touchet stopped struggling straight away, dumbfounded that his young passenger was armed and had landed him on his back so easily. Radisson tightened his stranglehold, half-smothering his captain and pushing him ever closer to the water. Touchet's back was pressed hard against the boat's side, his head dangling out into the void.

"I'll drown you," Radisson threatened him.

Touchet groaned feebly. "Have mercy!"

"Why? Now why would I have mercy on you? You're the swine! Nobody hits me, you got it? Nobody!"

Touchet remained precariously balanced between the deck and the water. Radisson held himself back, not wanting to cut his cheek.

"Now listen up, you brute," he snarled, shoving Touchet down nearer to the water, close to the point of no return. "Swear at me once more—once more!—or even look like you're going to hit me and I'll cut you up into little pieces and feed you to the fish! Nobody will ever hear from you again and nobody will ever know I was the one who cut you up. Am I making myself clear?"

"Yes, yes," gasped Touchet, half-strangled. "Just let me go."

"Now you're going to bring me to Orléans just like we said because you and I form quite the team, don't we? You're going to stay in your end of the boat at the helm and I'm going to stay up front. You keep your distance or else I'll put you on a spit like a chicken. Got it?"

Touchet nodded imperceptibly. But Radisson wasn't done yet. He shoved the captain overboard, catching him by the scruff of the neck as he fell toward the water. Slamming his body against the hull, he held him up by the throat with his forearm, the tip of his knife still pressed against his cheek.

"Didn't hear you. Do. You. Understand?"

"Have mercy," implored Touchet. "I'll do anything you ask."

"You'll bring me to Orléans?"

"Yes."

"You won't ever raise a hand to me again? You'll stop shouting at me?"

"I promise. Just let me get back to my feet now. Please. I'm frightened. I don't know how to swim."

"Just one more thing. You can see that your boat's still moving. It just needs a shove to set it on its way again. There was no need to hit me for that. So, if I let you come back on board, you can do the pushing. Then, as soon as the barge is free, you'll find a place nearby for us to spend the night. We won't talk about what just happened. Tomorrow morning we'll leave like everything's just fine. OK?"

"OK."

The confrontation had cleared the air between the two men. They barely exchanged another word, but worked together better than before. A night's sleep helped ease the tension. There was now sufficient trust between them. Circumstances had made them partners, not rivals. But they had nothing else in common.

In many places, navigating was tougher than usual. It had barely rained for two months and the further upriver they went, the lower the water level was. The river was much shallower than normal. Whenever the wind blew, they had to cast anchor so the current wouldn't sweep them out of the narrow channel they could navigate in. Then as soon as the wind looked like being back in their favour, they took off again, clearing bridges, weaving their way between sandbanks, and passing by villages until they reached Tours, where a difficult stretch had become impassable.

Carters were waiting for the boatmen, offering to tow their boats from the riverbank. Radisson jumped out onto dry land to find out more. Two carters, who seemed honest and well intentioned to him, advised him to unload the barrels and store them on their carts while they pulled to avoid damaging the bottom of the boat by dragging it along the riverbed.

Radisson went back to explain the situation to Touchet, who got out to speak with the carters himself. The captain knew there was sometimes no getting around this solution, extreme though it was, and decided both men were honest and knew what they were doing. The main thing was to get themselves unstuck, all the while handling his precious *Louve* with care. And the price seemed fair to him. The deal was sealed quickly

The two men pushed their cart out onto the riverbed to make transferring the barrels of salt easier. Radisson's strength was on show for all to see as he moved the barrels around with ease. Touchet gave him a hand, using a hoist fixed to the mast to lift them out of the barge. Once they had finished, Radisson stayed behind with the carters on the bank to watch as they stowed the merchandise and towed the barge. The irony was not lost on him that they were using the same technique as the Iroquois did whenever they had·to drag their canoes out of the water and past the rapids. To pass the time as they followed the four strong horses that advanced slowly before them, he told the carters how he had helped the Indians in Canada carry their birch-bark canoes along the riverbank in much the same way.

"You're from Canada?" asked the bigger of the two, his enthusiasm surprising Radisson.

"And what do you know about Canada?"

"The woman I work for has a cousin over there."

For the past fifteen years, the nun who had founded the Ursuline convent in Québec had been sending long letters to her family back home.

"She's always going on about it," added the carter. "She's completely obsessed."

It turned out that the lady was a great admirer of her cousin and all her work over in a country her letters described as dangerous and lacking in even the most basic necessities. Since the last worrying letter she had received, she was anxious to find out all she could about New France.

"You have to come meet her. She's never met anyone who's lived over there."

Without asking Radisson what he thought of his plans, the man had roped him in and was busy preparing his trip to the village. Radisson had no objections, but he feared Touchet would seize the opportunity to leave him behind.

"I'd love to," Radisson replied. "But my boatman will want to press on. I have to stay with him. I need to get to Paris as quickly as possible."

"I'll hear nothing of it!" the carter retorted. "Your boatman will stop with us too! The woman I work for will make him an offer he can't refuse! Believe me, he won't want to turn down a piece of business like this. Come on, Hercules. Come on, boy. Faster!"

As he urged his horses forward, the carter—Jean Roussin— began gesticulating over at Touchet. He was going to be making

BACK TO THE NEW WORLD

money hand over fist, he shouted. In fact, he was so convincing that, by the time the barge had been towed to a deeper stretch of water, Touchet was ready to drop anchor there and then and pay the lady a visit.

Roussin and his companion Thomas brought their new friends straight to their superior. Along the way, it began to rain heavily and they were soaked by the time they arrived. After parking the carts in the stables, where they would be safe and dry, they ran for shelter in the warmth of the big house.

The widow Guyard welcomed the two strangers with surprise. When Jean Roussin told her the younger of the two had just arrived from Canada, her face lit up and tears welled in her eyes. She looked at Radisson like he was an apparition of the Holy Ghost. Fascinated, she cupped his hands in hers as though he were some kind of marvelous creature. Radisson had no idea what to say to the griefstricken woman. She was in her forties and staring at him with fire in her eyes. Her astonishment passed and she quickly withdrew her hands to put them behind her back. She leaned forward with her head, humbly, as though she had just been indecorous.

"Do come in," she said. "Come dry yourselves by the fire. And please let me know when you are ready to eat."

The four men walked through an enormous kitchen, the widow just ahead of them. In one corner, a young servant girl was busy making dough for the next day's bread. Cooking pots hung above a long wooden counter that ran from the door to the fireplace. They huddled around the fire as the widow stirred it back to life, throwing an armful of slim branches down onto it. They went up in flames instantly, crackling noisily. She added a huge hardwood log. The woman reminded Radisson of how his mother had looked after him and how his sister Marguerite took care of him in Trois-Rivières when he stayed with her and her family. Mothers could be such a comfort.

The widow turned around. She only had eyes for Radisson, who was delighted to be the centre of attention. He could tell she was driven by a mix of embarrassment and curiosity.

"You need plenty of courage to live in New France!" she said. "I know that only too well: my cousin writes to me every year. She lives in Québec. She founded the Ursuline convent over there. She's a real saint to put up with everything she has told me about. Her name's Marie, Marie de l'Incarnation. Do you know her?"

"No, ma'am. I live in Trois-Rivières."

"Trois-Rivières!" the widow exclaimed, turning back to the fire to hide her emotion. "It's simply dreadful what happened there."

A lump rose in Radisson's throat. What could she be talking about? What terrible thing had happened? Judging by her reaction, it looked as though there had been deaths. But who had been affected? His sisters? Someone he knew? He was anxious to find out, but refrained from asking, not wanting to reveal he had not set foot in the colony for some time.

"Life goes on," he replied instead, genuinely moved.

He forgot all about his companions, who were eagerly eyeing the long table that awaited them in the next room. They were hungry. But this woman fascinated him, perhaps because her heart leapt along with his at the very mention of New France or because she had news of people he had met over there. He was anxious to stay by her side.

"Twenty-two dead," the widow added, her head down. "Not counting the prisoners. That's what Marie wrote to me last year. The Iroquois attacked the village, she said. They lured the French into a trap. They tried to free the prisoners, but it was too late. The Iroquois escaped with them. How terrible..."

"Yes, terrible."

Radisson was completely dismayed. More than the widow suspected. Distraught, he supposed his adoptive Iroquois father might have taken part in the slaughter. How had he ever become an Iroquois? Why had he ever chosen to fight by their side? It was hard to comprehend now that he was far from their lands. He was happy at least to have left them. As for the people of Trois-Rivières, he wondered how they recovered from such a thing. They were probably no more than a hundred now. What a blow!

"Thirty people lost," the widow added after a moment. "Just imagine what that must do to such a tiny village. You certainly need plenty of courage."

Catherine Guyard again looked Radisson straight in the eye, so emotional that it seemed she had come down with a fever. She was still under the spell of the strapping young man who, in her eyes, was the very embodiment of the whole colony, the faraway land she had so many times conjured up in her mind as she read her cousin's letters.

"I have so much admiration for Marie!" she exclaimed, her eyes lit up. "You know all about Canada. You understand me, I'm sure. She's earning her place in heaven every day, while the rest of us—"

"We all have our crosses to bear, too," interrupted Jean Roussin, who was now wondering if bringing the young man along had been such a good idea after all. "Life here isn't easy either, Catherine. You do your bit, and so do we."

New France was far away and things over there weren't all that rosy. Roussin was beginning to tire of hearing all about her saint of a cousin. Everyone had problems of their own. He had wanted to please Catherine by introducing her to the stranger. What wouldn't he do for the woman he hoped to marry? But he feared his plan might be turning against him.

Radisson was stealing his thunder and as Catherine ogled Radisson, talk had yet to turn to the big business idea he had in mind. He could see Touchet was beginning to grow impatient too, and he didn't want to let the chance slip through his fingers.

"Let's eat," he said.

The widow didn't hear him and went on. "This year, the Iroquois are everywhere, Marie wrote. They are massacring the French. They are burning the harvests. They are tearing the country apart. She says that even though the colony is under threat, she has no intention of returning. She is prepared to end her days over there. She is a saint, I'm telling you, an absolute saint."

Catherine lowered her eyes and blessed herself as she said a prayer under her breath.

"You, too," Roussin interjected. "You're a saint in your own way. Now, if you want us to send our wheat to Paris, it's time to sit down together and eat. Bring us some soup and come sit with us."

Radisson was shaken. So things had gotten worse since he had been captured. The fur trade had no doubt been brought to a standstill. But for the moment it was best to turn his thoughts from the project closest to his heart. The question was now to see if it was still worth returning to New France. Perhaps he could serve the Jesuits and help the people of Trois-Rivières, while waiting for things to improve. But never would he fight the Iroquois.

The two carters and Touchet were sitting at the end of the table nearest the fireplace. The heat and light from the fire reached them through a broad archway. Radisson reluctantly returned to his companions.

The Guyard home was big enough for employees to eat there, day or night. Carters, day labourers, and servants all had meals there, as well as the family. Catherine Guyard's husband had died ten months earlier and she had taken over the job of running the transportation company and the farm. Fortunately Jean Roussin and his brother helped her out. She wouldn't have made it otherwise. It had been a tough year.

Catherine served up a big bowl of soup, her face kept low. In her heart of hearts, she thanked God for sending her a real Canadian who had walked on the same ground as Marie. She almost felt as though she could reach out and touch her through this third party, that Radisson was bringing her closer. A fine-looking loaf of white bread landed on the table— the finest bread reserved for the big occasions—and Roussin got stuck into it, passing around a hunk to the rest of the table. It wasn't just the treat of white bread with no bran, rye, or barley to detract from the delicate flavour that left him more talkative than usual: he also hoped the boatman—who struck him as the grasping kind—would bring to fruition a plan he had been mulling over for several weeks.

Roussin reminded Radisson that news from Paris was very bad indeed. Thomas, who had stayed there until the fall, until the fighting had ended, said the city had become unlivable. He had chosen to return to his family in Tours because there was nothing to eat in Paris. The people who lived in its faubourgs said the wolf was at the door. Even in the city itself, only the very rich were able to eat. Unless things changed, a lot of people were going to die. Out of Christian charity, Catherine was keen to do her part. She planned to send grain so that the farmers could sow it in the springtime and harvest in the summer.

"Catherine isn't exactly rich and the harvests were nothing special here," explained Roussin. "But she thinks it's our Christian duty to help those in need. And I want to help her."

Radisson was speechless. The unrest had already started when he left Paris four years ago, but how had things gotten so bad?

"What fighting?" he stammered.

Everyone was surprised he had heard nothing of the unrest affecting much of the country.

"It's a real war zone!" Touchet exclaimed. "Have you been living in a cave or something? There's a war between the rebel princes who want to usurp the throne and those who are faithful to the real king! The country has been turned upside down."

"The soldiers have ravaged everything," Thomas chipped in. "Fields, animals, homes—they've pillaged and burned everything around Paris."

Radisson was fearing for his mother, who lived in the faubourgs.

"That's why bread costs an absolute fortune," Roussin explained. "But Catherine wants to give her grain away to the poor. The rich don't need her charity."

"The officers have kept all the money for themselves," Thomas continued. "The soldiers paid themselves by looting the wheat lofts, down to the very last grain. They set homes on fire to keep warm. They killed men for sport. They raped women. Things are bad there. Really, really bad."

Catherine kept quiet, while Radisson listened with dismay.

"Paris is dangerous," said Touchet. "There are thieves everywhere. I'd stay well clear of it, if I were you."

Roussin was disappointed to hear the boatman sum up the situation in such uncertain terms. He had thought the boatman was heading there. But he wasn't going to be put off.

"There's good business to be had for merchants not far from Paris. The bakers, it seems, have moved ten leagues outside the city. All to the same place. When their bread is ready, they come into town in an armed convoy to sell to the highest bidder. They're making a fortune and buying up all the wheat they can lay their hands on at sky-high prices."

Touchet was beginning to understand the piece of business the carter wanted to talk to him about.

"There's no way I'm gonna go get myself killed over there!" he exclaimed. "If that's why you brought me here, you got the wrong man!"

"Who said anything about getting killed?" Roussin replied, rubbing his hands together contentedly. "Any merchant worth his salt won't go as far as Paris. Charenton is where it's at. That's where the bakers buy up wheat at any price. They're far from the unrest; they're safe there."

"Too risky," Touchet replied, but this time sounding less sure of himself. "I'm going no further than Orléans."

"The bakers have thought of everything," Roussin insisted. "They have everything they need right by the Seine, far from the people who are starving to death. It's in your hands if you want to be just as rich as they are."

The lure of making a tidy profit started to nibble away at Touchet's doubts and he worked out how long it would take him to get there and how much money he could make. He at least wanted to listen to Roussin's offer. Radisson was also on the lookout, seeing that he could reach Paris easier than planned.

"Thomas and I," began Roussin, leaning in toward the boat-man as though telling him a secret in strictest confidence, "we'll come on board with you to hand out the wheat to who-ever we like once we get there. Thomas knows people we can trust, good people we want to help. We have more of the risk because we'll have to get the grain to their farms, but that's our problem. You've nothing to fear. You'd stop off in Charenton, sell your share of the wheat to the bakers, then wait for us for a day or two. Then you'd drop us off in Orléans, if that's fine with you, or bring us back to Tours. It's up to you."

"How much wheat would be in it for me?"

"I'm getting to that," Roussin replied. "Catherine and I would sell you half the wheat we can load onto your boat, at the Tours price. Judging by what we hear, you'd be able to sell it for three or four times the price in Charenton. What do you say?"

"I'm in!" interrupted Radisson. "You can count on me, Roussin. No harm will come to the four of us!"

Catherine cast an admiring glance at Radisson. In her eyes, he embodied the derring-do required to live in New France. But Touchet could have done without Radisson getting involved. This greenhorn wasn't going to decide if he was going to put his life and barge at risk on such an undertaking. Nonetheless, he was reassured to hear he could count on the daring young man who knew how to defend himself.

Catherine looked at her friend Jean. He was leading the negotiations on her behalf with such skill. She knew he wanted to marry her and was touched by his patience and perseverance while she was in mourning. He was even showing courage by taking this risk to remain true to his word. Touchet said nothing but seemed more and more interested. Roussin went on, encouraged.

"If we take the new Briare canal, we'll be there in less than ten days. I've a hard time believing you'd turn down an offer like this, Touchet."

The boatman pulled a face, hoping Roussin would up his offer.

"Tell me, what else can you transport at this time of the year to turn a profit like this? Catherine and I are even prepared to buy two barrels of salt to make more room for the wheat."

"Buy four," Touchet raised him, "at two *écus* each and we can talk about a price for the wheat. We'll see if it's as worth my while as you say it is. I'm still not convinced."

Radisson thought back to the many times he had sat in on haggling like this as his father reached a price with his customers. He enjoyed the tension as each party defended his interests and profit. The best price always went to the man with the most skill and tenacity. Judging by how little money found its way back to their home, his father seldom came out on top.

Roussin and Touchet were nearing an agreement. The boatman had wangled a concession or two more out of the carter, who was prepared to go no further.

"One *écu* per sack of wheat," countered Roussin. "That's already less than the Tours price. And the bakers will welcome you like the Messiah over there. You're about to make yourself a lot of cash, Touchet. Don't take advantage of a helpless lady who wants to do a good turn. That's my last word."

Touchet knew he wasn't going to get a better offer. But he was pleased. He had managed to sell four barrels of salt at a good price and would be able to transport twenty-five or thirty sacks of wheat for himself, making two *écus* on each. That more than made up for the risk of making the trip."

"It's a deal!"

Catherine was happy with how Jean had led the negotiations, and with the outcome. He would be able to get at least twenty sacks of seed to the poor peasants Thomas had known there. She could do no more to help them and ease her conscience at the same time. While Roussin went to fetch the wine that would seal the deal, she asked Radisson for a favour.

"Would you be so kind as to deliver a message to my cousin in Québec?"

"With pleasure."

The rain was falling so hard they had to wait a full day until they could load *La Louve*. Radisson spent a second night in the small room he had been given underneath the eaves. He tried to form a clear idea of what the future held in store for him as he listened to the rain drum against the roof. All things considered, the crisis that showed no signs of abating in New France hadn't dampened his desire to go back. But he felt more eager to serve the Jesuits. Trading was at a standstill and he would rather not fight, would rather not kill, again.

Three days of heavy rain had made the Loire easier to navigate. *La Louve* continued on to Orléans without incident. Touchet made a stop to unload the last barrels of salt and pay for the goods bought from the widow. Jean Roussin left the money behind with a merchant they regularly did business with so that Catherine could have it, come what may. Touchet also brought his young nephew and further provisions on board.

As they approached Briare, where the brand new canal opened up to join the Loire to the Seine, scenes of devastation became increasingly common. A rebel prince's army had passed through the area, his men behaving like foxes in the henhouse, pillaging and ransacking everything in their path. All along the shore, *La Louve*'s crew observed the ruins of a deserted hamlet in silence. Cow and horse skeletons littered the ground, picked clean by crows now retreated to the blackened beams of burned-down buildings. Things were looking bleak.

"Soldiers set up camp not far from here," explained Touchet. "They say they stayed barely two weeks, just time enough to take everything."

Radisson loved the new canal. The locks allowed them to easily negotiate the handful of small valleys that separated the two rivers. The days of transferring their goods on and off the boat were behind them. No longer would they have to make long journeys by cart. What a boon to trade! What a bold move it had been to create a new river in all but name!

As they neared the junction of the Seine, a menacing-looking young man appeared on the high embankment to their left. He was soon followed by three, six, then ten more of his companions, each eyeing the sacks of wheat piled high on the barge. Touchet ordered the crew to each take a stick and grabbed for himself the two long kitchen knives he had taken on board at Orléans. Jean and Thomas clutched the long poles they had picked out to keep would-be assailants at bay, pointing with them at the thugs as they hurried along the embankment in pursuit of the barge. Touchet's unpredictable nephew, who hadn't yet turned thirteen, twirled his club awkwardly above his head, more to reassure himself than to scare off the bandits, all of whom were bigger and stronger than he was. Radisson held in one hand a short stick similar to an Iroquois club and in the other a nicked kitchen knife Touchet had loaned him. If they attacked, he would use his eagle-head knife instead. He could already feel its reassuring presence against his skin. The powerful spirit within it reassured him that they would overcome this gang of thieves, even though they were outnumbered two to one.

"Look out!" cried Touchet, spying the robbers' leader working a slingshot.

A rock slammed into the barge. Touchet only just missed it by diving behind the freeboard. The other bandits sent a shower of rocks their way. The four men hid behind the sacks of wheat. No one had been hit. Radisson and Roussin countered, flinging back any rocks within arm's reach.

The gang disappeared for a moment behind the embankment. They reappeared further along and rained more projectiles down upon the barge, which the crew again only narrowly avoided. The thieves beat a retreat just as quickly as they had reappeared and repeated the manoeuvre three times without hitting anyone. After an hour of this game of cat and mouse, their attackers disappeared for good as the last lock approached.

That evening, Touchet dropped anchor right in the middle of the Seine and designated nightwatchmen to ensure the robbers would not surprise them. The night passed without incident and they left again early the next morning.

The rebel armies had been in this area for a while now. They went through a large village where everything had been burned to the ground. Of one hundred or so homes, nothing remained but wood frames and half-collapsed stone walls. A year had passed since the carnage and still no one had come back to live there. Radisson had never seen such complete and utter desolation. It reminded him of a story his father Garagonké used to tell him about the destruction of the Hurons. War destroys all.

The barge went by another pile of ruins, this time a small town surrounded by a wall that had not been able to keep the soldiers out. A few locals wandered around among the patched-up buildings. Thomas told them that here the soldiers had disembowelled the townsfolk after taking their homes and possessions. No one had ever seen the like of it. They raped the women then stuffed their vaginas with powder and blew them up. It made them laugh. The very thought of it sent shivers down Radisson's spine.

Two days later, they arrived without mishap in sight of Charenton. Once the barge had been secured near the bakers' camp, Radisson jumped out onto dry land to join a convoy headed for Paris. He took an *écu* out of his purse as he ran and showed it to a baker who let him scramble up onto his cart. He didn't turn round to wave goodbye to his companions. He had helped Touchet as much as the cantankerous boatman had helped him. Their work together was over now. The others had been nothing more than fleeting shadows. In the devastated world he was discovering, it was every man for himself. Paris was within reach. That was all that mattered.

Father Le Jeune was enjoying a break. It was a grey day and he was having trouble writing the *Relations*, Jesuit reports of news from New France based on letters sent to him by missionaries earlier that year. The jubilation of earlier days had given way to grave problems. His task was becoming harder and more complicated. But it was mainly the previous day's visit from Vincent de Paul that was weighing on his mind. A tireless man, he had come to ask Le Jeune to support his efforts to convince the Society of Jesus to do more for Paris's poor. Vincent had set up a network to aid the destitute, but it was not enough. He needed more money, more staff. The needs were tremendous.

Father Le Jeune left aside the documents that were piling up on his desk. Peering out his office window from the third floor of the Saint-Germain novitiate, he despaired at the sad state of affairs. The faubourg had been more or less spared by the opposing armies, but it was still in a real mess. The pain and the poverty were palpable. Vincent de Paul had reminded him that the hard times some had fallen on were unbearable. The Jesuit was eager to help these poor people. It was his order's duty, he said. Unfortunately, Le Jeune's cause was the missions in Canada, where things were scarcely better. And, in these troubled times, it was harder than ever to find money for the ambitious project. "Why so much suffering, Lord?" he asked himself. "Why so much suffering?"

He came back to sit down at his desk, picked up his quill and wrote a word or two. But his heart was no longer in it. From the pile of papers he had left on the desk, again he picked up the note a messenger from Amsterdam had delivered to him ten days ago. He read it again, trying to grasp its exact meaning for he could see very little hope between the lines.

Amsterdam, January 6, 1654
Father Le Jeune,

This brief note complements another I wrote last evening and that a young man by the name of Radisson will deliver to you shortly. In the note I entrusted to him, I recommend you take him into our service and assure you that he will be most helpful on our missions in Canada. I hereby confirm the sound opinion I have of the young man. Nonetheless, I urge you to be prudent. He lived for two years among the Iroquois and I know that he was fond of these barbarians. Let us be on our guard. Please ensure that the note he carries is still correctly sealed and keep a close eye on him for a while. Please take him in hand in the future. For even though I have returned him to the straight and narrow of our faith, I believe a relapse is still to be feared. You have laboured longer than I in Canada and will know what to expect. You will no doubt be able to exercise your perceptive mind and recognize in him either a faithful servant to our Society or an opportunist seeking to profit from our influence and our funds. Please be vigilant, I beseech you. May God help you.

Joseph Poncet

Le Jeune was now certain Poncet was the missionary the Iroquois had captured near Québec. His colleagues had told him about the capture in their letters. It had to be him. So the Iroquois had released him. Or Poncet had escaped... He wondered if it was a sign that the Iroquois' hold on the colony was slipping at last. Otherwise, why the gesture of goodwill on their part? Nothing in the note shed any light on the matter. If the Iroquois had freed Poncet, there was hope that things in New France might be improving. But was that really so?

As for Radisson, try as he might Le Jeune couldn't find any trace of him, in his memories or even in past correspondence. He had never heard tell of the young man. He was eagerly awaiting his arrival, hoping that he might be able to tell him more about the Iroquois' state of mind. For him and many other French settlers in Canada, the nation remained an enigma. He also hoped Poncet's first note would be clearer.

The Jesuit inspected the note again to be sure he had not missed any information in the margins or on the back of the page. But no, he had read every word of it. He read it again carefully.

He began to think its author might be slightly unbalanced. Perhaps Poncet had undergone a traumatic experience at the hands of the Iroquois. It was possible. One thing was clear, though: Poncet was free, and that was encouraging. The Iroquois had not killed him like Father Brébeuf and Father Lalemant. Objectively, there was cause for hope.

As a precaution, he warned all the Jesuit institutions in Paris of Radisson's impending arrival. It was an event he did not want to miss.

Giving free rein to his imagination, Le Jeune was suddenly struck by how the news had reached him. The image of the Dutch rider handing him the message, exhausted, barely coming down from his horse at all, his clothes dusty, with his long black riding boots and his old feathered hat... The coincidence got him thinking about a theme for the retreat he would be leading the week before Easter.

Hope was sometimes born of the most curious circumstances. That's why, even in the darkest moments, even in the face of situations that appeared to be devoid of all hope, as when Christ had been crucified, one had to keep the faith and continue to pray, for God was almighty and always looking down over his flock.

|||||||||||||||||||||||||||||||||||||||||||||||||||||||||||||||||||||||||||||||||||||||||||||

CHAPTER 4

DEVASTATION

NEVER WOULD RADISSON have imagined such devastation. He didn't recognize the faubourg Saint-Antoine where he had grown up at all. Once fertile fields all lay fallow, overrun by thistles and worthless hay. Stone houses looked like bodies with their clothes torn off. Soldiers had ripped out all the wood they could find—doors, windows, shutters, frames, furniture, ceilings, and floors—to throw on their fires. They had broken up the frames with axes. Roofs had disappeared or fallen in. Windmills had lost their sails. Wooden homes had been taken apart. Only a handful of solid stone buildings belonging to religious orders and aristocrats, protected by surrounding walls, had resisted.

Radisson continued on towards the family home. The area had changed so much that he was having trouble finding it. Along the way, he passed by people repairing their homes. Others, emaciated, seemed to have given up and were wandering aimlessly, staring blankly ahead. Beggars held out their hands as he walked past. He was so stunned, in such a state of disbelief, that he did not even see them. He arrived at a crossroads where locals had found the strength to take their fate into their own hands. Artisans were at work in their boutiques.

An almost empty store had opened its doors. The small block of houses was finding a new lease on life. Not far from there, Radisson recognized the road that led to his home.

There it was. That was their family home. Or at least what was left of it. It had been reduced to a deserted square of masonry, completely disfigured, with no doors or windows. A piece of the roof hung down over the front wall and onto the road; another had fallen inside the house. There was not a soul to be seen. Inside or out. Feeling completely helpless, Radisson stood there paralyzed, his arms by his sides as he surveyed the ruins of his childhood. He looked around him. Where was his mother? For hundreds of feet in every direction, no house had been spared. Nothing. All around. Discouraged, he went to sit inside the ruins on a pile of rubble that had fallen off the fire-place. How would he ever find his mother? What could have happened to her? Had she taken refuge somewhere? Radisson feared she might be dead.

He felt lost.

An old woman shuffled over towards him, bent with age, wrapped up tightly in any number of shawls to protect her from the biting wind. Radisson walked over slowly to meet her. She stopped before him, trusting him completely, raising her head to look the big, strapping lad in the eyes.

"Excuse me," he asked. "Would you happen to know what happened to the people who lived here?"

"They left," she replied. "As you can see."

Her voice full of sympathy, she recounted how some of the people who lived in the faubourg fled to Paris before the fighting, taking all they could with them. Others stayed to protect their possessions. It hadn't been a wise move: they had perished with everything they owned.

"I used to live here," Radisson chipped in. "I'm looking for my mother."

"I can't help you, young man. Some were fortunate and got help from family or friends. I didn't know any of them. I live in a hut over there," she said, pointing. "There are a lot of new folk around here now, not all of them honest. Can't tell you any more than that."

Radisson concluded that he should maybe take a look around Paris. Perhaps he should ask at the rare customers his father did business with inside the walls, but he would have trouble finding them again. He had only been there two or three times. His mother had never come with them. So how could she have taken shelter with them then? It would be like looking for a needle in a haystack. But he had nothing else to go on right now. The emptiness around him was bringing back painful memories of his father's disappearance before Radisson left for New France. His whole family had been broken up, scattered to the four winds.

The church was over there, still standing. His mother would go to mass there almost every day. Perhaps the priest had helped her make her escape, perhaps some of the nuns she knew had sheltered her in a convent.

Over at the church, a priest he did not know was handing out bread to dozens of paupers gathered around him. The old woman he had spoken with earlier was among them. Many were horrendously thin and dressed in rags. They shivered with cold and hunger. Radisson stayed to the side, waiting for the priest to stop handing out bread. He then went over to ask what had become of the parishioners, mentioning his mother and a few neighbours by name. The priest did not know. He had been helping the poor in the faubourgs for only a few months. He had heard that many locals had died here during the fighting. Rumour had it that the previous parish priest had been killed too, when the first army arrived and his church was requisitioned to house the officers. He had stood up to them and been killed. The priest was keen to continue his rounds and wished Radisson the best of luck. Radisson went back to the crossroads, hoping to find something to eat.

"Any bread?"

"Any money?" the merchant replied warily.

"Yes," said Radisson.

"How much? Prices are up this year."

Now it was Radisson's turn to be wary. Another man, sitting behind him in a corner, was watching him. He still had twenty *écus* in the purse Poncet had given him, hidden under his clothes. It was a lot of money. He would rather no one knew he was carrying so much around. So instead he rummaged in his pockets and held out thirty *sol* coins in the palm of his hand.

"That's not enough," the merchant grunted.

Radisson wasn't in the mood to be turned down.

"I'm hungry! Give me something to eat for thirty *sols*! And be quick about it!"

The storekeeper decided it was best not to try to outsmart this tough character who was becoming more threatening by the minute. He went into the backstore where the bread was hidden and gave him half a loaf.

"That's all you can have for thirty *sols*."

"That's fine. Thanks."

It was enough to satisfy his hunger. Radisson walked out of the store with the loaf hidden under his jacket. He ate away at it as he wandered around what had been his family home, trying to come up with a sensible strategy to find his mother. He wanted to at least try. There was no way he was giving in right away, slim though his chances were.

At nightfall, he slipped inside what remained of his home to spend the night there. He hid himself away under the fallen-in roof to be safe from bandits, beside the fireplace he and the rest of his family used to eat in front of. It was cold. Luckily he still had his wool jacket. But he couldn't fall asleep. He felt bad for having left to follow his sister Marguerite to a distant colony, never to return. She had had enough of being told what to do by her father and the parish priest. Their father disappeared shortly after that. Then the priest had recruited Françoise to serve the Jesuits in the same village as Marguerite. His mother had cried for days. And he in turn had given in to his craving for adventure and had left, too. Their mother, home alone. Defenceless.

He tossed and turned.

As soon as the sun rose on the horizon, Radisson set out for the centre of Paris.

At Porte Saint-Antoine, the fighting had left its mark on the walls of the Bastille. The bank of homes rose up and struck Radisson like a smack on the mouth. He had forgotten just how huge and densely populated Paris was. It was like walking into an enormous forest of stone that was inhabited by thousands of people. As he trudged up the street, on each side extravagant stone churches and clusters of high homes stretched as far as the eye could see. But the lingering stench of excrement gave the impression that he was walking through a giant outdoor stable. It was noisy, too: carriage wheels rumbled, horses neighed, street peddlers shouted, a crowd of people made a racket on their way by. He could see the mark the violence had left on the city. Things seemed less exciting to him than when he used to go there with his father. But here there was more of a recovery underway than in the faubourgs.

People thronged around a convoy of bread. Hired men protected it from protests against the price hikes. The bakers turned a deaf ear to the pleas and handed over their precious bread only to those who could afford to pay.

Tired and confused, Radisson didn't know which way to turn in the huge city. The staggering number of streets and homes had taken the edge off his determination. Any direction might be the right one, but none seemed particularly promising. There were no clues to help him decide. He tried to imagine his mother's reaction, if she had indeed come into Paris to find shelter. But no flash of inspiration came to mind. She had no relations in the city. She had followed her husband from Provence to satisfy his ambitions. Religion was the only reason she might have gone somewhere in particular. His mother was a very pious woman. She might have taken shelter with a religious organization. But which one? There were so many of them.

Three- and four-storey homes towered over Radisson on all sides. He looked for the belltowers sticking out over the rooftops. He saw three and headed toward the tallest, to his left. He stopped in front of a colossal church by the Seine, but was too intimidated to go inside. He didn't have the strength to start asking priests he didn't know if they happened to know Marie Radisson from the faubourg Saint-Antoine. He did not believe in miracles and his efforts seemed destined to fail. He did, however, promise himself he would go into churches further on, later on, and pray for God's help.

He came out into a large square and stopped in front of the city hall, fascinated by the impressive building's stone façade, entirely sculpted as though made out of wood. A carriage pulled by four frisky horses suddenly appeared out of nowhere. Radisson dived out of the way, only narrowly managing to avoid it. The golden coach pulled up in front of the city hall's main door. The four horsemen escorting it pushed back the crowd. "Out of the way! Let us through!" they cried from their saddles. Radisson retreated further in case one of the horses stepped on him. "Out of the way!" cried the horsemen as they dismounted to push back onlookers with the flat sides of their swords. A man armed with two pistols stepped out of the coach and stood next to it. He pointed his weapons at the Parisians, who looked on in fright.

Radisson, who didn't appreciate being pushed about, was furious at having had the cold metal of the sword pressed against his chest. He kept one hand on the eagle-head knife hidden under his clothes, ready to retaliate, although he knew it would be too dangerous to confront the escort of a powerful lord, particularly the armed valet. He struggled to put a cap on his anger.

A footman wearing a sumptuous silk jerkin dismounted. He opened the door to the carriage with a bow as an extravagantly attired man got out. The arrogant-looking count, duke, or marquis was wearing a broad-brimmed black hat adorned with white feathers and a curly brown wig whose locks tumbled down over his shoulders. A cape cut from scarlet cloth half-covered his gold-embroidered jacket, which ran down his arm to his broad lace cuffs. His pantaloons, also made of lace, resembled a woman's skirt, and his long square-tipped shoes boasted broad golden ribbons that made it difficult to walk. Radisson was taken aback by such a display of riches in the midst of such poverty. The powerful figure disappeared as quickly as he had arrived behind a heavy, finely carved door of the city hall.

The horsemen then went about dispersing the crowd. "Get out of here! You have no business here!" Radisson didn't wait to be asked twice. He wandered off, bringing his uneasiness with him, leaving the Seine behind as he took to smaller streets lined with more modest homes, where there was less chance of coming across another aristocrat.

Where should he look now? He glanced up at the sun to gauge what time it was. It must have been around noon. Without any real conviction, he gave himself a few more hours to find his mother. He walked blindly through narrow streets that cut across each other to form a confusing maze. He cut a random path, remembering that he had vowed to go into a church. But church steeples were less common in this neighbourhood. A tall, gaunt man suddenly stood in his way.

"Looking for something?"

Three more men surrounded him. He had allowed himself to be surprised by thieves, like a halfwit.

"If you have money, we can help you," added the ringleader facing him.

"I don't have a *sol*," Radisson replied curtly.

"Give me your jacket then. That will do me for today."

The tall man stared him down as the three others jostled Radisson to shake him up.

"Give me your jacket! Be quick about it!"

Radisson stiffened and took a step back. He didn't want to give in to the threat because if he handed over his jacket they would see he had money. The ringleader took out his knife.

"Hand it over or I'll cut you to pieces!"

"Now the fun begins," the thief to Radisson's left whispered into his ear.

"I'll be scraping your insides up off the street in no time," said the thief to his right.

The third man punched him hard in the back. A shiver ran down Radisson's spine. He was afraid he might be killed. He was sure the ringleader wouldn't think twice about carving him up to see what he had on him. He had to defend himself.

"Let me be!" exclaimed Radisson, trying to sound as anxious as he could manage. "I have money. I'll give you everything."

"Good. Now we're talking. Stand back, lads. Watch as he hands over his money to me."

His tactic worked like a charm. Radisson used the moment of respite to take out his knife.

"You think you're gonna frighten me with that?" laughed the ringleader, getting ready to attack.

But Radisson charged at him, shouting his Iroquois war cry at the top of his lungs. He cut through his shoulder into the bone and the man fell to his knees, moaning. The fight was over for him. Radisson turned to the three remaining bandits, still rooted to the spot at the sound of his fearsome cry. They each ran off as fast as their legs could carry them. Radisson chased after the man who had been looking forward to tearing his guts out, swearing he would pay for the others.

The man ran quickly, though, and knew the neighbourhood well. He tried to lose Radisson in the maze of tiny streets, but an Iroquois can keep going for longer than any Parisian and Radisson was sure he would catch up to him. He was gaining on him, brandishing his knife when the spirit of his father Garagonké intervened: "Follow the path of peace, my son." And so, instead of striking him, Radisson shoved the man in the back. He fell flat on his face. Radisson put the brakes on, ran back to where the man was lying, and knelt down over the thief. He grabbed him by the hair, pulling his head back and threatening him with his knife.

"Have mercy," pleaded the man, shaken by the fall.

Radisson hesitated, bringing the blade of his knife down onto the man's throat, carried away by a thirst for revenge, then checked by the spirit of Garagonké: "Your way is the way of peace, my son." He brought his knife to the man's brow— the robber was crying now—and pressed it where his hairline began, exactly where the Iroquois would scalp their victims. He made a long cut, then buried the thief's face into the ground, hissing at him: "You don't deserve to live, you rat! But a powerful spirit is watching over you. You can thank the heavens I'm sparing you."

Radisson walked away. None of the onlookers dared intervene. Further on, he rinsed his knife in a public fountain and put it back in its sheath. He walked towards a belltower, entered the church, and knelt down before the altar. "Lord, forgive me for my sins. I only wanted to defend myself. Protect me from hatred and help me find my mother." But he had given up on the possibility and asked the priest how to get to the Jesuits. He followed the very precise directions and found their college, where he was told Father Le Jeune was not there. He was off leading a retreat at the Saint-Germain novitiate. The Jesuit speaking to Radisson had the presence of mind to inquire after his name and immediately recognized the long-awaited traveller. He explained how to get to Rue du Pot-de-Fer.

It was a long way. Radisson took the Pont Neuf and crossed the Seine, walked past the Basilique Notre-Dame-de-Paris, then crossed another bridge. There he lost his way, tracked back on himself, looked for his bearings, asked for directions, and finally ended up, exhausted, in front of the Jesuit novitiate just as night was falling. A high stone wall stood between him and the buildings. He banged louder and louder against a locked door, yelling, "Open up! I have an urgent message for Father Le Jeune! I have come from New France!" He shouted until the porter at last let him inside, anxious to avoid a scene. When the young man showed him the crumpled note from Father Poncet, the porter, who had been expecting him, beseeched Radisson to calm down and led him to one of the rooms set aside for travellers, promising he would be able to speak to Father Le Jeune the following day. Radisson collapsed onto the bed, completely worn out.

Although disappointed at having to interrupt his Holy Week retreat, Father Le Jeune was so looking forward to meeting Radisson that he left the faithful to pray alone for a while.

The meeting took place in his office.

Radisson was struck right away by the aura of serenity given off by Father Le Jeune. Being in his company calmed him down immediately. He remained silent for a long time to let the feeling of peace wash over him. At last Paris had a nice surprise in store for him.

Le Jeune was in no rush to break the silence either. He took a good look at the newcomer, trying to gauge whom he was dealing with, beyond what Poncet had already told him. His first impression was favourable. The young man seemed a little troubled, but likeable, and he had no doubt he had what it took to work in the difficult conditions of New France.

"I have a message for you," Radisson said eventually, handing over the crumpled parchment he had been carrying since Amsterdam.

Le Jeune took it, feigning surprise.

"Father Joseph Poncet asked me to deliver it to you in person. I crossed the ocean with him. From Manhattan. We parted ways in Amsterdam. I promised him I would come meet with you and talk about Canada."

Le Jeune was pleased by Radisson's honesty. It confirmed Poncet's first message, which he had reread before the meeting.

"If I may," the Jesuit replied, "I will take a moment to read the message and we shall talk after that."

"Go right ahead, Father."

First and foremost, Le Jeune ensured the envelope's seal had not been broken. It had not, despite the parchment's poor condition. A point in Radisson's favour. He opened the letter, keeping a discreet eye on the young man's reaction. Radisson's thoughts appeared to be elsewhere.

Amsterdam, January 5, 1654
Father Le Jeune,

Please receive this young man, Pierre-Esprit Radisson, with open arms. He escaped the Iroquois at the same time as I and we travelled together from New Holland to Amsterdam. He lived among them for two years. He is familiar with their language, their customs, their strengths, and—I hope—their weaknesses. I have managed to convince him to serve us in New France, where his knowledge will be of great assistance to us. If he appears before you within two months of this day and delivers this letter still sealed, I have accurately judged his character and he is someone we can trust. Welcome him as my protégé and please see to it that he returns to New France without delay.

Joseph Poncet

Although brief, this letter showed more conviction than the first. Father Le Jeune nevertheless noted that his colleague did not appear to have been freed by the Iroquois; it seemed he had escaped. Hopes of a peace with these terrible foes in the near future faded. But other matters were of greater concern. Before looking up again to speak to Radisson, the Jesuit allowed himself a moment of quiet reflection, pretending to still be reading. The message clearly indicated that Poncet had already recruited the young man, even though Poncet appeared to have been in some doubt just a few hours later when he wrote the second note. Perhaps Radisson had not given a firm commitment. There was still work to be done then. Comparing

Poncet's letters in his mind, Le Jeune drew three conclusions. Radisson's strong suit was his knowledge of the Iroquois. It was up to him to make sure the young man could be a reliable servant to the Jesuits. He would also have to decide if there was a need to apply Poncet's advice: "Keep a close eye on him and take him in hand in the future."

"Father Poncet tells me you know the Iroquois well, that you wish to assist our missionaries in New France. Is that correct?"

Radisson was not expecting such a frank assessment. He remembered having promised Poncet to come talk to Father Le Jeune. Nothing more. But a lot of water had flowed under the bridge since then. Now the only thing he was certain of was his desire to return to New France at any price. If he had to serve the Jesuits to get there, he was prepared to go that route.

"I do know the Iroquois well," Radisson replied. "I lived among them for two years. I speak their tongue. I know their customs. I promised Father Poncet I would come talk to you because he believed I might be of use to you. If you would like my help, I am prepared to work for the Jesuits in New France. As long as I don't have to kill any Iroquois."

Father Le Jeune was taken aback by this unexpected remark.

"Whoever said anything about killing them?" he retorted. "The cross of Christ is our only weapon. Our intention is to convert them, not to go to war with them. Wherever did you get such an idea?"

Radisson was sorry the emotions of the past few days had gotten the better of him. But he recalled that tensions were running so high in Trois-Rivières when he had been captured that everyone, including the Jesuits, was on the offensive against the Iroquois. He believed he was right to bring the matter up since he would prefer not to get involved.

"I know there are Iroquois who want peace," he added. "That's what matters to me."

"Very well!" exclaimed Le Jeune. "We both want the same thing. Do tell me more about these peaceful Iroquois. Do you really think peace is possible?"

"Before I left the Mohawks, an Onondaga delegation came to talk to them. Peace was in the air."

"Encouraging... Listen, I do not yet know you, but you certainly inspire confidence. I'd like to tell you a secret. Or rather, a rumour. In the last letter I was sent from our missionaries in Canada, they told me the Iroquois have proposed a truce. A number of our countrymen are skeptical and fear it may be no more than a ploy. Do you believe the Iroquois are acting in good faith?"

"Probably. Anything is possible with the Iroquois. If it's peace you're after, I can help. Send me back to New France and I will serve your missionaries faithfully. I will never give them reason to complain."

Father Le Jeune settled back into his chair. He admired the young man's attitude, even though he sensed a rebellious streak. He wondered if Radisson would be able to manage the strict obedience that members of the Society of Jesus owed to their superiors. Also, the closer he looked, the more he seemed to be hiding something.

Radisson was in a hurry to leave Paris, to put his decimated family behind him. Since he had set foot in the calm and clean surroundings of the novitiate, where everything had its place, he was feeling better. The Jesuits could be his new family. He knew they were influential and well organized in New France. He could hardly go wrong by teaming up with them. When the fur trade picked up, he would see where he stood then.

"Honestly," Father Le Jeune went on, "I feel you are committing yourself a little too hastily. You do not even know what we expect of you."

"I know perfectly well, Father," replied Radisson, quick as a flash. "Father Poncet explained everything."

"I see," said Le Jeune, surprised at his assurance. "All the same, I would still like to get to know you a little better. For instance, how much time did you spend with the Iroquois? What were you doing there?"

Radisson would have preferred to avoid the question. Either he gave a frank and honest answer and risked being judged severely by the Jesuit, or he lied and managed to get away with things for a little longer. But never could he erase what he had experienced among the Mohawks. Sooner or later the question would come back and bite him.

Le Jeune looked him square in the eye, his gaze remarkably clear and piercing. He was a good man. Radisson could feel it. He even felt as though he was in the company of someone truly exceptional. He wanted to tell him the secret he had buried away since he left America. But first, he took a precaution or two.

"Is it true you lived in New France?" he asked.

"I worked there for seventeen years!"

"Do you know the Indians well?"

"Of course. The Innu and the Algonquins best of all, but I was also with the Hurons. And I met the Iroquois on a number of occasions."

Radisson could see compassion in the Jesuit's attitude. He decided to tell him the truth.

"The Iroquois captured me three years ago. They tortured me. Then they adopted me because of my courage. My father and brother thought I could become a good warrior and I became one to honour them. I killed a number of Erie on an expedition that lasted eight months. The Iroquois in my village respected me for that. But some were jealous. They never forgot that I was a Frenchman. A few wanted to kill me. That's why I fled. I met Father Poncet with the Dutchmen, where both of us were hiding. I told him everything. He forgave me. I'm sorry for killing innocent people. I am a man of peace now. I would like to get into business, too. Like my father."

So that's it, Father Le Jeune said to himself. He was a little taken aback by the turn of events. One hour ago, he had still been meditating with a group of devout Parisians and now here was a young man suddenly reminding him of the colony's tremendous difficulties, the failed Huron mission, the financial missteps… He would need more time to ensure the potential recruit would be able to serve the Jesuits while respecting their rules and principles. Nonetheless, something told him Radisson would serve them faithfully and would be a big help in New France. But two questions wouldn't leave his mind.

"Are you aware you cannot do any trading if you agree to serve us?"

"Yes. But the trade is at a standstill at any rate. And, as far as I can remember, the Jesuits relied on the fur traders for help, didn't they?"

"In a way, yes… And if the Iroquois attack our missionaries, if their lives are in danger, what will you do then?"

"I will defend them, Father, like I was fighting for my own life. It's not the same when my life or the lives of my masters are at stake. I won't have to think twice about it, believe me."

Le Jeune was reassured.

"You do know this is Holy Week?"

Radisson nodded, although this was news to him.

"At the moment, I am leading a retreat for around one hundred people. I would be delighted if you joined us. Praying for a day or two will do you the world of good. You can take the opportunity to examine your conscience and we'll be able to get to know each other better."

"As you wish, Father."

"Very well. After the retreat, if we both still agree, I'll send you to La Rochelle. You will arrive in time to take the boat with the fishermen who often deliver letters and parcels for us to Île Percé, where they fish. They are men we trust. From there, you can easily make your way to Québec. What do you say?"

"Perfect."

Father Le Jeune stood up.

"I have a favour to ask you, Father. I tried to find my mother, Marie Radisson. She lived in the faubourg Saint-Antoine. But our home was destroyed and my mother left. If ever you could help me..."

Le Jeune did not dare respond right away.

"Unfortunately," he said at last, "the worst atrocities were committed in that very faubourg. Many left their lives there."

"My mother was very devout. Perhaps she took refuge with the nuns."

"Perhaps. I'll see what I can do. But I'm afraid you shouldn't hold out too much hope. My advice is to pray with all your heart for the duration of the retreat. Your mother is surely in need of your prayers, wherever she may be."

PART III

IN NEW FRANCE

||||||||||||||||||||||||||||||||||||||||||||||||||||||||||||||||||||||||||||||||||||||||||||||||||

CHAPTER 5

FALSE START

O NCE AT PERCÉ, Radisson found a small boat to take him to Québec. Along the way, he was struck by just how wild Canada was: there were trees, mountains, coves, and rivers everywhere. There wasn't a soul to be seen before the trading post at Tadoussac where the Indians came to trade furs with them. After a rest day, the *Marie-Anne* went on. More trees, mountains, coves, and rivers until Île d'Orléans outside Québec.

Who wouldn't be moved at the appearance of the small settlement at a bend on the St. Lawrence? Radisson was no exception. It was a heartwarming sight as a hundred or so homes at the foot of Cap Diamant and a few larger buildings on top of the cape came into view.

As soon as he reached dry land, Radisson walked up Côte de la Montagne to meet the Jesuits' superior in New France. Father Le Mercier gave him a warm welcome in his roomy residence. After reading Father Le Jeune's letter to him, Le Mercier asked Radisson to report to Father Paul Ragueneau in Trois-Rivières without delay. Ragueneau would know how best to use him. Radisson also took the opportunity to ask if his sisters were still alive. They were.

He boarded another boat. The last homes at Cap Rouge were behind them. For two more days, the shores of the St. Lawrence were completely bare: no French buildings, no Indian villages, only trees and the mighty river they were making their way up, a pathway paved by the sun.

The village of Trois-Rivières came into view. Just a few cables more and Radisson would be back to where he had started. Sails tacked, the boat glided along until it reached the shore. Radisson had been waiting for this moment for so long and was the first to jump ashore. None of the five men who watched them arrive recognized him. They didn't suspect for an instant that the young man who had disappeared three years earlier could be back. Everyone was sure he was dead, killed by the Iroquois.

"What's this, Michel?" a well-built Jesuit cried out from shore. "Your boat looks pretty much empty to me."

"I did what I could, Father. I have rope, knives, and tools for you."

"The devil take you!" the priest replied impatiently. "If it goes on like this, I'm going to have to go get everything I need myself. Show me what you have then."

Radisson intervened.

"Excuse me. Are you Father Ragueneau?"

"The very same."

"I have two messages for you, Father. One from Father Le Mercier in Québec, and the other from Father Le Jeune in Paris."

"Paris?" inquired the Jesuit, surprised.

Radisson handed him the letters and he opened Father Le Jeune's immediately. He had not seen him in years, although he regularly sent him progress reports and letters.

The young man who handed you this message has under-taken to serve the Jesuits in the colony. The Iroquois captured him near Trois-Rivières three years ago and he is well versed in their language and customs. He should be of use to you...

Help at last! Father Ragueneau looked up enthusiastically.

"You couldn't have come at a better time! What's your name?"

"Pierre-Esprit Radisson."

"Seriously? You're the brother of my servant Françoise. Everyone thought you were dead."

"That's me. I'm Françoise and Marguerite's brother."

"Well, what a turn-up for the books! Your sisters will be overjoyed, believe me! Go find them right away. We can get to know each other later, back at the residence."

Ragueneau had made quite the impression on Radisson. He couldn't have been more different to the weak and sickly Poncet. The young man hurried to the gate in the stockade that ran around the village. It was wide open.

What a strange sensation it was to see the thirty or so tiny wooden homes huddled together, the steeple from the modest Jesuit chapel towering over them. There was hardly a soul left in the village. No guard watched over the entrance. The relaxed atmosphere contrasted sharply with the situation Radisson had known three years earlier.

He grew excited at the sight of Marguerite's house. He burst in without knocking, ready to surprise her, but she wasn't there. He walked around the house and found her out back, hauling a heavy bucket of water up from the well. As he walked up to her, his heart beating so hard he felt it might jump out of his chest, Marguerite turned around and saw him. She stood rooted to the spot, thinking it might be Radisson. After a moment of incredulity, she was certain: it really was her brother, back from the dead. She dropped her bucket and ran to take him in her arms. They hugged each other. Marguerite was crying with joy.

"My brother," she sighed. "My little brother."

She took a step back to make sure she wasn't seeing things. But it really was Radisson, in one piece and alive and well. Still stunned, she cupped Radisson's face in her hands.

"Where were you? What on earth happened to you? For the love of God."

Radisson couldn't muster a reply. He could still hear Marguerite's last words to him: "Whatever you do, don't go wandering off from the fort." So much suffering could have been avoided if only he'd listened to her. So much time had passed since. He was so happy to have found her again. Still unable to speak, he held her close. They embraced again, in silence.

"Everyone thought you were dead! What happened to you?"

Radisson took Marguerite's hand and led her over to a bench beside the back door.

"It's a long story" was all he managed to say.

He fought back tears as he smiled at her with all his heart.

"The Iroquois adopted me. I lived with them for two years. Then I ran away. I had to go back to France before I could get back here… I'm so happy to see you!"

"Me too! I was so angry at myself for letting you go!"

"No, no, it was my fault. You've nothing to feel bad about. Nothing would have happened, if I'd listened to you. It's all my fault."

Marguerite's oldest boy, now four, walked out of the house. He came and hid himself in his mom's skirt, sensing that something out of the ordinary was happening. He looked up at Radisson with big questioning eyes. Inside the house, the youngest howled, but Marguerite didn't seem to hear him.

"They tortured me. But I got through it."

"The main thing is you're alive," she said.

"And how are you? How's your husband?"

Marguerite held her son tight.

"He's dead. The Iroquois killed him in an ambush, scalped him along with twenty others. I'll never forget how he died."

Radisson remembered the story the widow Guyard had told him.

"It was all the French commander's fault. He didn't understand how things work here," Marguerite continued. "He ordered them to counterattack the Iroquois. They were running away after attacking us. But it was a trap. Everyone here suspected as much. We knew we shouldn't go out. Véron obeyed his orders, just like the others. Twenty-two dead, all told. The French commander included. It was tough. But things are picking up now. There's peace again."

"With the Iroquois?"

"Yes. No one knows why, but you won't hear us complaining. Last summer, first they went back on the offensive, then, from one day to the next, it was peace talks they wanted. Pierre Boucher and then the Jesuits took care of everything. Father Le Moyne was really great. Now they're busy working on a big mission to the Onondaga. That's practically all anyone's talking about."

Radisson couldn't believe it. How times had changed since his capture! Nonetheless, he was in no hurry to talk about his past as an Iroquois warrior. Those who lived in Trois-Rivières, and even his own sister, would never forgive him.

"I've been thinking about remarrying," Marguerite went on. "A woman can't stay a widow long around here. We need children and plenty of them if we're going to see better days."

Radisson was a little taken aback.

"Anyone in mind?"

"Médard Chouart. He went off last summer with Indians who had allied with the French. Far from here. It's a really dangerous trip. We can't be sure he's ever going to come back, but I'll wait for as long as it takes. He's the man for me, the man I chose."

"He's off trading?"

"Maybe. The Indians he went with still want to trade with us, even though they're far from the Iroquois. But no Frenchman has ever set foot there. It's so far that Médard wasn't sure he would be able to bring back any fur. But he wanted to go so as to stay in their good books. Médard is so brave. I trust him. And while we're waiting, this year everyone is tending the fields because trade is at a standstill and the Iroquois have finally left us alone after stopping the harvests for two years. It was really tough, Pierre. You can't imagine how hard it was. Lots of people died, so much suffering. But things are looking up now that you're back."

"It wasn't easy for me either, you know. I'll tell you all about it."

The brother and sister fell silent for a moment, lost in thought. There was so much to catch up on, so much to tell each other. Radisson didn't want to bring up their mother's disappearance, though.

"What are you going to do now?" asked Marguerite.

"I'm going to serve the Jesuits."

"You? Work for the Jesuits?"

Marguerite would never have pictured her brother working for a religious order. He had always been a bit of a rebel. Like her. The polar opposite of their mother and their sister Françoise. She had a hard time getting her head around how her brother had managed to survive his time with the Iroquois.

"You should go find Françoise," she said. "She's having a hard time of things, too. She's changed a lot. You'll see."

Radisson found his other sister cooking in the Jesuits' big kitchen. He didn't want to startle the most fragile member of the family and so he stood back in the doorway. She kept her back to him, thinking that a Jesuit brother or father had just come into the room. But after a moment she realized that a stranger was waiting to be seen to and she turned around. She too froze as she thought she recognized her brother. He seemed more mature and headstrong, hardier, more muscular. But he was looking at her with a glint in his eye, as though he knew her. She couldn't believe it was him, and yet... Suddenly she fell to her knees, her hands joined in prayer, and thanked the heavens.

"Jesus, Mary, and Joseph, and all the saints," she whispered. "Pierre? Is that really you? My brother?"

"It's me!"

She picked herself back up. He walked over to her, swept her up in his arms, and held her tight. He twirled her around as Françoise sobbed uncontrollably.

"Thank you, dear Lord. Thank you. It's a miracle."

Radisson set her back down. They gazed at each other, their hands clasped. She had changed a lot, he thought. She was now a woman. She was pretty and had a good figure, was less frail than she had been before.

"How are you? Marguerite told me things haven't been easy around here..."

"Not at all!" Françoise replied, wiping away tears. "Lots of people have died. And we've been so terribly hungry. But things are getting better now. And yourself? What happened to you? Where on earth were you? The Iroquois didn't kill you like the rest?"

Radisson told her of his misadventures, without mentioning his life as a warrior. Instead, he stressed his talents as a hunter, which had meant he had been spared. Françoise sat down with him at the big table and neither spoke much. Being together again, in good health, and filled with the hope of better days to come was great consolation for everything they had been through. They had never been particularly close, but that day the feeling of being reunited as a family was hard to beat.

Soon it was time for Radisson to meet Father Ragueneau, the man whose orders he would now be following. He left Françoise, promising they would see each other very often now, without further explanation.

He went into the next room, which doubled as Father Ragueneau's office and storage room. The Jesuit was opening one of the crates that had arrived that morning from Québec.

"Be seated. I'm almost finished," he said. "I imagine your sisters were delighted to see you again."

"Yes, Father. They were very, very happy."

"And what great news! Françoise told me of your disappearance. Everyone thought you were dead along with your two friends. It was just that we had never found your body. But by the grace of God, the Iroquois spared you. More often than not they give no quarter. Just like this peace that has come down upon us from heaven. A true miracle! Did your sisters tell you we were at peace?"

"Marguerite told me, yes."

"And that's the very reason why I need you. Please, sit down."

The Jesuit moved aside a roll of bark that was blocking one of the room's two chairs. They sat facing each other, on either side of a small pine table.

"Father Le Jeune tells me you are now in our service. Our superior believes it is here that you will be of greatest use. Is that so?"

"That's how I understand it."

"Perfect. I need some help preparing an important mission among the Iroquois. Did you ever travel with them?"

"Yes. I went on long canoe trips with my family."

"You speak their language?"

"Fluently."

"Excellent. Your knowledge will be a big help to us. But, first and foremost, I must make sure Father Le Jeune told you all about our way of working. You know we are a little like an army? You must obey me like a soldier follows his commander's orders, just as I must obey Father Le Mercier, my superior. The system is a simple one, and it works well."

"So I was told."

"I want you to help me prepare the expedition. This Iroquois mission will be just as important as our mission among the Hurons. We will be staying with the Onondaga, who invited us. Are you familiar with them?"

"A little. I stayed with the Mohawks."

"Of course. The nation that never tired of attacking us. It stands to reason they were the ones that captured you. The Onondaga appear to be less threatening. They are asking us for missionaries and we are not afraid to send them. They have become real allies. Father Le Moyne has been living with them for one year now and he is sure they are acting in good faith."

"In the final days I spent with the Iroquois, an Onondaga delegation came to my village specifically to talk about peace."

Radisson was careful not to add that the delegation had been poorly received by the Mohawk leaders.

"The most surprising thing," Ragueneau went on, "is that peace came about overnight. A revelation! When Father Le Moyne took the chance to go with them last fall, some believed it was a ploy. I myself was very suspicious. But they really did have a change of heart. That's why we need to seize this opportunity and settle among them in numbers. As you might well imagine, there is a great deal to prepare. You really couldn't have come at a better time."

Ragueneau's enthusiasm enthralled Radisson. He had been listening to him for barely five minutes and already shared his assurance and verve.

"This is what I expect of you: While I take care of the skeptics who still doubt this mission's importance to the colony and gather together the remaining funds, you will begin packing. Put together everything we'll need with Brother Leboeme—I'll introduce you shortly—and your sister Françoise will take care of the food supplies. We must be ready to leave within a month. That doesn't leave you much time, granted, but you'll manage. Provided you start today!"

Radisson wasn't sure he would be able to shoulder the responsibility Ragueneau had suddenly thrust upon him before even getting to know him, but he vowed to do everything he could to rise to the challenge.

"Follow me now. I'll show you to your room and introduce you to Brother Leboeme. Then we'll go to the smith. He's going to have his work cut out."

News had spread like wildfire around the village: one of their own had disappeared and was back home, safe and sound. The Iroquois hadn't gotten him. Lots of people stopped by to congratulate Radisson on their way back from the fields. The next day a party was thrown in his honour, a real feast washed down with plenty of eau-de-vie.

While Ragueneau made his way to Québec to try to gain the governor's support for the mission, Radisson began putting together the materials required to build and equip the fort the French would build among the Onondaga. The Jesuit had given him a rough list. The smith, Charles Aubuchon, would make the hinges, latches, locks, racks, and other ironware that would make the fort invincible. He would need to work non-stop to get everything done on time. Radisson would have to have more iron sent from Québec to cover the huge order. What's more, Aubuchon would also have to sharpen and repair any tools that were already available: drill bits, blades, planes, handsaws, and pit saws would all be needed for their construction work.

It was enough to make them wonder if the colony was ready to take on such an ambitious project.

As Radisson met with people to get everything he needed from the list, he realized that many locals disapproved of the expedition. The merchants especially were against it and refused to provide the goods they would need to trade. They didn't trust the Iroquois and thought there were many other matters in the colony that should be seen to first. Starting a building site on the other side of the world made absolutely no sense to them. When Ragueneau returned from Québec with the good news—the governor had agreed to fund part of the project—he had to meet with them to try to bring them around.

The meeting was held at the Jesuits' residence. Trade had been so slow that three of the four merchants there had now completely turned their attention to farming. The fourth, Michel Langlois, was kept busy transporting goods on his boat between Québec and Trois-Rivières, usually for the Jesuits. Despite the very warm July weather, Ragueneau insisted on keeping all the windows shut so that the conversation would remain private.

"I don't understand you," Ragueneau told them. The Jesuits have always paid you cash on the barrelhead! You'll get your money back as usual, in no more than a year. There is no risk, I can assure you. Why are you being so stubborn? What's the problem?"

None of the merchants wanted to be the first to answer: the Society of Jesus held too much power in the colony for anyone to go up against it.

"Things are moving too quickly," Langlois at last decided. "Once your fort is ready and you're sure the Iroquois want peace, then will come the time to trade with them. But until that time, it's just too risky."

"But trade has ground to a halt! Things aren't looking too good for you these days. Here I am giving you the chance to at last make a little money and you're telling me you'd rather wait! Wait for what? The Second Coming? You'll be ruined long before then! And the colony with you!"

"Michel's right," Noël Racine chimed in. "The trade goods aren't going to lose their value. Provided they stay here with us, there's nothing to fear. After all that's happened, Father, surely you can understand we have reason to be wary of the Iroquois. They asked you to send missionaries, so go ahead and send them, if that's what you want. But we'd rather wait a while before we start trading with them."

"You know very well the Iroquois trade a fortune's worth of furs with the Dutch. Once we are in their lands, we will try to convert them while others try to turn part of this fur trade to our advantage. If we have nothing to offer them in return, the Iroquois will continue to make the Dutch richer and we'll keep on getting poorer. Nothing ventured, nothing gained, gentlemen. It's a well-known fact. The Jesuits are investing a fortune in this enterprise and we expect you to do your part. The whole colony stands to benefit, starting with you."

The four merchants looked at each other, sweating and uneasy, but standing as one. Radisson had been following the discussion discreetly, preferring to stay in the background, and he knew very well that they hadn't dared tell the priest what they really thought, opinions they had shared with him on more than one occasion. The merchants dreamed of making the project smaller, reducing it by at least a half, and delaying it as long as possible. In a perfect world, they would have liked to see it cancelled completely.

"Bringing a mission to the Iroquois is the best way to get trade going again," declared Ragueneau. "We're going to turn things around in our favour! The more confidence the French have in themselves, the greater the show of strength, the more the Iroquois will respect us. At last we have a chance to prove we can replace the Dutch! All we need to do is sell the right items at the right price. Gentlemen, this opportunity is not to be missed! Unless you have any better ideas?"

"Think about Médard Chouart," countered René Hunault. "He set off a year ago and no one's seen hide nor hair of him since. Maybe he's dead by now, all his wares lost forever. If we wait a little longer, maybe we'll see that trade is going to pick up on that side."

"We salute his courage. Let's hope nothing has happened to him. It's a big risk he took for the common good. But no one knows what shape our former allies are in. We do not even know where they fled to escape the Iroquois. Médard Chouart had no guarantee he would be able to bring back any furs. My proposal, on the other hand, is a sure thing: we know where the Iroquois are, we know their intentions, and we are sure their trade with the Dutch is substantial. If we bring them a great many goods to be traded, we will bring back many furs. It's simple mathematics. And so I expect you to take part rather than run away and look for cover."

"I don't trust them Iroquois," René Huault replied. "It's too risky."

"They're our allies now!" Ragueneau exclaimed, his face red with the heat and the strain. "Are you afraid? Is that it? You'd rather hide away like our nuns shut up in a cloister? God bless their souls... What I'm saying is there's no point waiting around, or even praying—we have to act! As our founding saint taught us: pray as though everything depended on God, but act as though everything depended on you! What sort of businessmen are you anyway? You ought to be ashamed of yourselves! Even the governor is behind our project. He's giving us a great deal of money to move ahead with it. You'll be left behind, and too bad for you! We'll just have to find other partners."

"Wait, Father," intervened Claude Volant, who had not yet spoken. "Stay calm. Only fools vent their anger. We're ready to do our share... It's just that we're as poor as Job since the fur money dried up. All we have left is the merchandise you're asking us to put up with no guarantee. The Iroquois killed our brothers just last year, Father. Perhaps you've forgotten that. Well, we haven't. Why not meet halfway? Why not pay us for half the goods up front with the governor's money? The other half you have can have on credit. That way, the risk will be shared. That's only fair, isn't it?"

Ragueneau bit his tongue. Claude Volant was a God-fearing man, a man he had a lot of time for and a responsible, level-headed officer of the militia. The priest was also aware he should try to keep his temper in check; his anger had already landed him in enough hot water as it was. He took the time to calm down and realized that Volant's proposal was full of common sense.

"You can't let us down, Father," Volant added. "It wouldn't be fair to freeze us out. Think of the people of Trois-Rivières who have given their lives. The money we are asking for is going to be spent here, right here in a village very much in need of it."

Volant had cut in at just the right time, with solid arguments. Radisson thought Ragueneau should accept the compromise on offer. If his new master was a man of sound judgment, as he believed him to be, he would agree.

"You're right, Claude," the Jesuit conceded. "What you are suggesting is entirely reasonable. If you get paid for some of your goods now, you'll be less concerned. And all of Trois-Rivières will benefit. I am prepared to compromise. I'll see to it that you get half the money for your wares before we leave, provided that you lend us the other half."

Radisson was pleased. But the merchants, who had not entirely gotten what they had come for, had to make the best of the situation.

Radisson admired the daring behind the project, which was built on the say-so of two Jesuits who lived among the Iroquois. Even though he sometimes defended the project to its opponents, he preferred to keep in mind that he was only an employee and was there to serve the Jesuits. The thought helped him get through the drawn-out negotiations.

The project took up all of his time. He planned, discussed, worked, and ate with Ragueneau, Brother Leboeme, and Françoise. And, when he wasn't doing that, he was running from one end of the village to the other to fetch this or that. Together with Claude Volant, who spoke Algonquin fluently, he asked the fifteen or so Indians who had chosen to live close by the village to build them the four birch-bark canoes they still needed. They agreed. Along with the fourteen canoes Radisson had used his powers of persuasion to mobilize in Trois-Rivières, that would be enough to transport the fifty men along with all the goods.

So that they wouldn't be entirely dependent on hunting and fishing, Ragueneau insisted they bring along plenty of food supplies. They would be spending many months there before a first harvest of vegetables and cereals. Thirty sacks of wheat from France soon arrived from Québec. Françoise had already reserved the pig and chicken couples they would bring with them to reproduce. She also salted vast amounts of pork and beef, sealing them in small barrels.

The smith who would be going with them arrived from Québec on Michel Langlois' boat, along with all his equipment: tools, anvil, fire tray, and bellows. He also brought with him the extra iron they had requested. Radisson had a double layer of bark cover the bottom of some of the canoes to protect them when carrying all the heavy materials. He divided the goods carefully between the canoes, making sure not to overload them.

Ragueneau was pleased with Radisson's work, but demanded the pace of preparations be stepped up. He wanted to be completely ready by the time the Iroquois arrived.

Brother Leboeme took care of the packing. One after another, he made little bark or wood boxes, filling them with knives, axes, and pots to be traded, as well as iron tools, pots, and kitchen utensils for the fort, lead for the muskets, and a metal supply. He took great care when packing the precious portable altar, liturgical vases, holy books, and the pious images the Indians enjoyed. The Jesuits would have all they needed for their apostolate.

Radisson and Brother Leboeme devised a packaging they considered to be entirely watertight for carrying the gunpowder in. They covered the powder barrels with waxed cloth and a double layer of bark. As for the sacks of wheat and peas, since there was no more waxed cloth, they dipped some strong cloth in the liquefied spruce gum the Indians used to seal the seams of their canoes. Now, even if it rained, even if the canoes took on water, not a single seed would sprout. It was vital their food supplies reach their destination intact.

Other items were less fragile. Radisson and Leboeme tied up rolls of cloth to be traded and placed glass pearls and little bells in jute bags without further ado; coils of rope went at the bottom of the canoes.

The toughest task of all had been finding new muskets. Ragueneau was determined to offer them as gifts to impress the Iroquois. Radisson had found only two in Trois-Rivières and none at all in Montréal—the colony's poorest French settlement—while merchants in Québec insisted on holding on to theirs. Ragueneau was first helped by Pierre Boucher— Boucher was always keen to support the Jesuits of Trois-Rivières and happened to be in the good graces of the governor in Québec—then he wrote personally to the governor, asking him to lean on the merchants.

And so twelve more new muskets at last arrived from Québec, along with twenty or so soldiers from the garrison, who were to protect the fort. Missionaries Ménard, Dablon, and Frimin arrived by boat two days later, accompanied by Father Brouet and Father Boursier, a mason, and three carpenters. Hot on their heels came the Jesuits' superior, François Le Mercier, the expedition commander, Zacharie Dupuys, and the interpreter, Guillaume Couture, who had already spent four years with the Iroquois.

The village of Trois-Rivières had never seen the like of it; people and goods spilled out of the Jesuits' residence and into the courtyard. Radisson gave up his room to Superior Le Mercier and slept outside, more comfortable there than in the house, as long as it didn't rain. Those in Trois-Rivières who still doubted the expedition's success were won over by the excitement in the air. Nobody dared criticize a thing. Although exhausted by so much going back and forth, the tension, and a sleepless night or two, Radisson managed to do everything Father Ragueneau expected of him. He and the merchandise were ready for adventure. The Iroquois could come.

On the morning of July 30, thirty emissaries beached their canoes in front of the fort in Trois-Rivières. Seeing the almost naked Iroquois land, their powerful bodies painted bright colours, Radisson was almost overcome with fright. Trying to make himself see reason, he thought back to the day he had fled his village. Back then, he had been terrorized by the thought of meeting an Iroquois, who would have killed him on the spot. This same nightmare was slowly resurfacing.

Commander Dupuys, Ragueneau, Pierre Boucher, and Pierre Godefroy, captain of the militia, came out immediately to greet them, followed by a handful of locals who milled around the foot of the palisade to take a closer look at their former enemies. As soon as Radisson regained his composure, he went out to stand with Marguerite, who was having a hard time containing her rage before the men who had killed her husband.

Once the emissaries had gathered around a large fire in the middle of the village, discussions commenced. The Iroquois were very surprised to see so many Frenchman ready to return with them; they had come only to discuss when and where their new allies should join them on their lands. They had no mandate from their chiefs to bring the French back with them, they said. The Jesuits insisted. The Iroquois resisted. The tension mounted.

It took two days for Guillaume Couture, who had perfect command of their language and a sound grasp of their customs, to appease them. Father Le Mercier had come to doubt their sincerity, even though, since Ragueneau had already organized everything, he was keen to leave immediately. Surprised he could still understand the Iroquois language so well, Radisson sat in on all the negotiations. From time to time, scenes of his torture would come back to haunt him. Whenever that happened, he would walk away for a time, returning to make up his own mind about the Iroquois' real motives.

On the third day, Guillaume Couture withdrew with the Jesuits, Commander Dupuys, and the experienced Pierre Boucher to tell them he was running out of arguments. He suggested they give the emissaries an ultimatum; he sensed they were close to giving in. The Jesuits approved of his strategy. Back with the Iroquois, Couture spoke in no uncertain terms:

"Enough talk. Either you take us to your lands now, as the people from your nation who came to Trois-Rivières before you promised us, or the Iroquois are liars and the French will never settle among them. The French have only one word, but the Iroquois have several, it seems. It's up to you. That's all we have to say on the matter."

The chief leading the negotiations asked for a little time for the Iroquois to discuss the matter among themselves. When they all returned to sit with each other, their spokesperson declared that they agreed to meet the French demands.

"Prepare your canoes and your bags, bid farewell to your women and children, for we will guide you to our country as soon as you are ready. The Iroquois also have only one word. The French are our allies and we wish to be at peace with them. You have prepared carefully in response to our invitation and we do not want to disappoint you. The responsibility of satisfying your desires rests with us."

The sun had set some time ago when Radisson, still not entirely reassured, raced back to inspect the bags one last time by torchlight. He was surprised to find himself shaking again, as though an evil spirit had crept inside him and taken hold of his courage.

During this time, François Le Mercier asked Father Ragueneau to follow him into one of the residence's closed rooms. The two men shut themselves away in the attic, with only a candle for light.

The two men could barely stand each other. Because of his intransigent, quarrelsome nature, Le Mercier feared that Father Ragueneau might try to rally everyone against the Jesuits. Two years earlier, he had written about the matter to the Society in Rome. The decision came down one year later, by return mail. Ragueneau had been removed from his position as superior, with Le Mercier taking his place. Le Mercier had sent him to Trois-Rivières immediately, wanting to sideline him and give him cause to consider his behaviour. Ragueneau had reluctantly obeyed, all the while continuing to come up with initiatives such as this expedition. He now feared this little tête-à-tête was going to mean more trouble for him.

"I don't like the Iroquois' attitude," Le Mercier told him. "Even though they have agreed to lead us back to their lands, it worries me they were so reluctant."

Something wasn't right about their attitude. But Ragueneau was quite certain his superior hadn't pulled him aside to state the obvious. He waited for more.

"That's why I think it would be wiser if one of us stayed behind. I mean a man of experience who will be able to act quickly, and make the right decisions, if things turn sour over there. I think that man should be you, Father Ragueneau."

The Jesuit gritted his teeth.

"I know what you're thinking," Le Mercier went on, "but you're wrong. It's not another punishment. On the contrary. Given the level of risk, we must be able to count on a man such as yourself. Father Le Moyne and Father Chaumonot are both over there and well positioned to advise us how to act. You will be most useful here. It's for the good of the Society, Paul. We'll be safer if you stay in Trois-Rivières."

"My experience would be more useful with the Iroquois, I'm sure of it..."

"Well, I need you here," Le Mercier concluded bluntly. "I order you to stay here. And you have no choice but to do what I say."

Despite the anger that flooded over him to the point that it made him dizzy, Ragueneau fought to keep a cool head. If he answered back, his fate would be sealed and Le Mercier would send him packing to France. Perhaps that was even what he secretly hoped for, but Ragueneau had no intention of giving him the satisfaction.

"Very well," he said in a voice devoid of all emotion. "But if I stay behind, I want Radisson to stay too. You have Guillaume Couture. I want to keep Radisson. I need someone who knows their language and customs. Otherwise I will be of no use to you at all. At least give me that."

"I agree," Le Mercier replied, happy to soften the blow he had just dealt his colleague. "It's a wise precaution on your part. It was very clever of you to think of it so quickly. Ask him to teach you the Iroquois language over the winter and, all being well, you can come join us next summer."

Ragueneau gave Radisson the bad news first thing the next morning. Although stunned and disappointed, he was also relieved because, try as he might, he had not been able to explain away his fears overnight. That said, he did not have the faintest idea why Ragueneau had had such a change of heart. Ragueneau wasn't about to tell him and quickly withdrew, visibly overwhelmed. Radisson still had trouble blindly obeying orders.

He helped load the canoes all the same. After a last furious day of labour, the eighteen canoes, loaded until they could carry no more, left the shoreline at last, heading west one by one, the three Iroquois canoes leading the way. The load was so big and the crew numbers so reduced that even the Jesuit priests were paddling. They formed a long trail out on the water, stretching almost as far as the eye could see, pointing like an arrow toward the horizon, making for a splendid, heart-rending spectacle. Radisson couldn't help but regret he was not part of the trip.

Standing on the shore, Father Ragueneau and he did not utter a word. The *habitants* come to bid an uneasy farewell to friends and family had gone. Ragueneau and Radisson remained until the last canoe had disappeared behind the spit of land marking the entry to Lac Saint-Pierre.

Slowly, they walked back towards the village, deep in thought. One was thinking of the day when he would leave to convert the Iroquois, the other of when his next chance to explore unknown lands would come along.

"I promise we'll both go to the Onondaga next summer," Ragueneau told him before they crossed back through the village palisade. "My place is there, with you."

"I'll be only too happy to, Father."

|||||||||||||||||||||||||||||||||||||||||||||||||||||||||||||||||||||||||||||||||||||||||||||||||||||||||||||

CHAPTER 6

TIME PASSES SLOWLY

RADISSON ADMIRED THE COLOURFUL FORESTS that stretched into infinity on either side of the beautiful Saint-Maurice river. Short days and cool nights had seized the land, cloaking the leaves in shades of yellow, ochre, and red. The bright autumn light cut through the bracing air.

Radisson was overjoyed to dip his paddle into the clear waters of the river, keeping the brisk pace set by Pierre Godefroy at the back of the canoe. He still did not know why the captain of the militia was in such a rush, or why he had insisted on bringing Radisson with him. Every time he found himself with Godefroy, Radisson felt guilty for bringing about the death of his son François. Since Ragueneau had ordered him to go hunting with him, he had no choice but to get over the uneasiness he felt. But given the speed they were travelling at, Radisson was sure they were not going hunting. "We have to go up the Saint-Maurice" was all the captain had told him.

At day's end, Godefroy steered the canoe into a small sandy cove, where they prepared to spend the night. Their makeshift shelter would be a comfortable one. The bed of balsam boughs was covered in beaver pelts. The fire was burning nicely.

"I've been keeping a close eye on you since you came back," Godefroy told him after the meal. "You've changed a lot in three years. You've become a man."

His mind put at ease by these words, Radisson was waiting all the same for some harsh remarks about his son's death.

"I've seen a lot of expeditions leave Trois-Rivières, but none as big as the one you prepared for the Jesuits. Nice work!"

"I did what I could. Father Ragueneau was pleased."

Pierre Godefroy threw another two dead branches onto the fire with hands as broad as paddles. He positioned them carefully, without saying a word. The lively flames lit up a face creased by deep wrinkles. He had untied his long brown hair, which now fell down over his shoulders.

"I've seen a lot of men die, too," added Godefroy.

Radisson stared at the fire to avoid his gaze, sure that he was going to be chided for being so irresponsible.

"Men I loved... Marguerite probably told you about last summer's massacre. I was wounded when the commander ordered them outside to counterattack the Iroquois. Many of us knew it wasn't the right thing to do, but the commander was too young, too arrogant. He'd just arrived from France. He got Claude Volant to hold the fort with me. There were thirty of us inside with Boucher, the only one who'd refused to go. The twenty-one who left with the commander were killed in an ambush. Not one man came back. I'm lucky to still be alive today."

Radisson felt a pang of sadness as he listened.

"I lost two sons, both to the Iroquois. François was with you when they surprised you. He's dead and you're alive. One day you can tell me what happened. But you need to be made of strong stuff to live with the Iroquois for two years and come through it. I admire you for that. You must've impressed them."

126

Radisson couldn't believe it. He had expected to be blamed, accused, lambasted for causing François' death. And quite rightly so, in his book. That day he had acted like the French commander who thought he knew better than the experienced men of Trois-Rivières, better than the Iroquois.

"I'm glad you're alive," Godefroy went on. "For us in the village it's like you've come back from the dead. Everyone thought you were a goner. It gives us all hope. It shows that God hasn't completely turned his back on us yet..."

Radisson was so stunned he didn't say a word.

"I'm not like the Jesuits, you know. I don't see everything as being black or white. You must have done a thing or two wrong for my son to end up dead. But what point is there holding it against you? It won't bring my François back. The Iroquois killed him, not you. And, even them, despite all they've done to us... I must admit they have some good customs."

Radisson was struck by the captain's strength as he forgave him and didn't condemn all the Iroquois as a whole, just like he had learned to by living among them and seeing their good side. He had not expected such wise words, such kindness, from him. Perhaps this man might understand why he had become an Iroquois for a time.

"The custom they have of adopting prisoners, for instance. That's a good one. It's generous of them to sometimes spare their lives. That's what happened to you, from what I've heard."

"They did adopt me. That's true."

Only the crackling of the fire and the rustling of the leaves disturbed the night. Godefroy didn't speak again for a while.

"I'd like to do what they do. If you agree, I'd like to adopt you as my son. You'll replace François, in part. It will make up for it. I'm proud of you. Do you understand?"

Radisson couldn't manage a reply.

"I'm not bitter. There's no point. It's best we are reconciled. I know you're as sorry he's dead as I am. We'll be able to get through it together. Because our troubles are not over. If you ask me, this peace with the Iroquois won't last long. Just like I told Father Ragueneau before I brought you up here with me, we need to stand together or else we're lost. I need you. The whole village needs you. And I can help you. That's why I want you to become my son."

Indescribable joy swept away Radisson's fears and remorse, just like when his Iroquois family had saved his life. He was never going to turn down the chance to become the adopted son of one of the most respected men in Trois-Rivières.

"I'd be only too happy to!"

The pace set by Godefroy still gave Radisson the impression of urgency. He didn't know why, but he trusted the captain— his new father—well enough to follow him without question. It had been a long time since he had felt so happy. Radisson paddled hard, never once complaining that they ate only at sunrise and sunset, that they never stopped. It was like being on a war expedition with the Iroquois. He was cut from the same cloth as the captain.

On the second night, as they ate, Godefroy opened up some more.

"The Jesuits haven't told you the whole story, you know. They haven't told you the peace is limited."

Radisson was surprised to hear what Godefroy was implying.

"When Father Le Moyne came back from among the Onondaga last fall, he confirmed they really wanted peace, even though no one believed them. But the story doesn't end there. The Iroquois wanted something in return. In order for other missionaries to go to their lands, they demanded all our former allies be excluded from the peace. I'm sure Ragueneau never told you that."

"No," Radisson confirmed, still unaware of the implications. "He didn't tell me that."

"The Jesuits aren't exactly telling anyone who will listen that they've become the Iroquois' lackeys. The peace is only for the French. The Algonquins, Hurons, Amikouès, Montagnais, and Etchemins, all our allies, are still at war with the Iroquois, who are attacking them while we stand back and watch. It's almost as if they're trying to provoke us! The Jesuits agreed too quickly. They wanted to get in the Iroquois' good books, or have a grand old time leaving on a mission to Iroquois country, but didn't stop to consider the consequences. Many of us think they were wrong. Now our allies feel betrayed. They're angry at us."

Now Radisson understood the situation better, even though he wasn't sure he shared the experienced captain's opinion. The fur trade the Jesuits were trying to get back on its feet with the Iroquois was important too.

"The colony is weak. Things have gotten worse since you left. It's a certainty that if the Iroquois had kept on attacking us, we'd have had to go back to France. We were at breaking point. That's why the Jesuits gave in right away. But it was the time to resist, negotiate hard, stand up tall! Now the Iroquois know we're at their mercy. You know why they offered us peace?"

Radisson shrugged his shoulders.

"And you spent time with them. Perhaps you have a better idea than we do."

Radisson thought back to all he had seen and heard when he lived with the Mohawks.

"I know the war killed a lot on their side, too. That was a worry for them. My adoptive mother and other people she admired in the village didn't think things could go on like that. She was hoping for peace."

Radisson didn't want to say any more. The Iroquois were divided on the matter and there were bound to be lots of reasons, both for and against, that were unknown to him.

"It's true things can't go on like this," Godefroy continued. "Did you see how much this big expedition cost? Why go running headlong into a project like that when the colony is still lacking everything? It's risky—the Jesuits themselves admit it. It makes no sense at all. There are so many more pressing things to do first before we start sending missions to the Iroquois!"

Godefroy was clearly one of those opposed to the mission. Until now, the Jesuit point of view had seemed the stronger, more constructive argument in Radisson's eyes. But he hadn't known that many old alliances had been sacrificed to get to this point. Now he wondered which side was in the right.

"Ever since the Jesuits decided to start a new mission that was just as big as the one they lost among the Hurons, but in ten times less time, they've raised a lot of hackles. They're hiding things from us. Even from me, and I'm in charge of keeping everyone safe. They won't follow my advice any more, or the advice of the experienced people who have always supported them. They just do as they please. Damned Jesuits!"

Godefroy stopped talking before his anger got the better of him. Radisson felt as though he was stuck between a rock and a hard place. He had been sure he was acting for the good of the colony by supporting Ragueneau. Now he wasn't so sure.

"Can I trust you?" Godefroy asked him.

"Of course you can."

His new adoptive father stared hard at him, weighing his maturity more than his sincerity.

"Here's the thing," he said. "There are more than a few of us in Trois-Rivières who think the Jesuits are making a mistake. Our allies had to flee far to the west to get away from the Iroquois, in part because we left them defenceless. We left them without firearms when they asked us for them. I'm with Médard Chouart, who's trying to find them. If these Indians abandon us, the Iroquois will wipe us out like they did the Hurons, Neutrals, and Erie."

Radisson felt a twinge of regret as he recalled the victories he had taken part in over the Erie, who had defended themselves without iron or muskets. Many Iroquois from his village had wanted to go back and fight them to cover themselves in glory.

"You know the Iroquois well enough to know how strong they are. They offered us peace from one day to the next. But they might turn against us just as quickly. They're the ones who decide. Not us. That's why we need to keep up our old alliances. But the Jesuits and the governor don't understand."

Godefroy was not wrong. Radisson himself had chosen not to stay among the Iroquois to escape with his life. But what could he do now that he had given his word to serve the Jesuits?"

"Tomorrow we meet the Algonquins who came to trade furs last week in Trois-Rivières. I have arranged to meet with them in secret. They live far to the north now. They are distrustful of us. As you saw for yourself, there are only fifteen or so left near the village. There used to be a hundred. My mission is to rekindle the alliance with them, even though the Jesuits are against it. I ask that you don't breathe a word to Ragueneau. I need your word on that."

Radisson hated being put in this situation. Did he really have to take sides? Was there not a way he could stay loyal to both at once?

"I brought you with me so that you can see what's really going on," Godefroy added, seeing Radisson's discomfort. The Jesuits are pulling the wool over your eyes. They haven't been honest with you. If we are to help the colony, everyone needs to be involved in the decisions. The Jesuits failed with the Hurons and they're probably going to fail with the Iroquois because they're not learning from their mistakes. There are a few of us in Trois-Rivières, Québec, and Montréal who think we need to be doing things differently. You'll soon see just how unhappy the Algonquins are. But I'm going to try to salvage our alliance with them. I need your word that you'll keep it a secret."

"I agree. I won't say a word. I promise."

Seven Algonquins were waiting patiently for Pierre Godefroy at the foot of an enormous waterfall. They had a great deal of respect for the captain from Trois-Rivières who had always been close to their nation. Together, they had signed a number of agreements to the benefit of both the French and the Algonquins. They had fought side by side. The previous summer, Godefroy's eldest son had gone hunting with one of their bands when the Iroquois had attacked without warning. They had fought and died together, brave and standing together right to the end. But the Algonquins they were meeting with were angry. They had gone to Trois-Rivières for powder and muskets and the French had turned them away, not wanting to displease the Iroquois.

The first thing Godefroy did was offer them a small barrel of powder. To thank him, the band chief Penikawa gave him the leather headband he had been wearing around his forehead. Then they climbed the path to the top of the waterfall, put their canoes back in the water, and went back up the river at great speed. Radisson had trouble keeping up with the men who had learned to paddle at the same time they learned to walk. It took four days to reach the Algonquin camp, where three huge drainage basins met at the source of the Saint-Maurice.

Surprised to see two Frenchmen arrive among them, the camp's residents gave them a cold welcome. Penikawa had to go around each teepee, reminding everyone that the French captain's eldest son had died fighting by their side. Godefroy took the chance to hand out small gifts to each family: a handful of metal needles, glass pearls, iron scrapers. Radisson watched the captain closely, noting how he established a rapport with them.

"With the Indians, you have to give in order to receive," Godefroy explained. "That's their custom. I wish I could have given them more, but I had to be careful Ragueneau wouldn't suspect something was up."

Megiscawan, the camp's most respected chief, knew Godefroy well from having lived a long time near the fort in Trois-Rivières. He had even taken part in the talks when the Iroquois had spoken of peace for the first time over a year ago. All the French allies had been included then. Megiscawan said he was happy to see his friend again, but appalled at the French U-turn. He nonetheless agreed to listen to what Godefroy had come to tell him.

The next day, in the large teepee reserved for ceremonies, Godefroy unpacked a long-barrelled musket, which he gave to Megiscawan. He set it down before the four chiefs on a red blanket spread out on the ground and added a nice-looking eagle feather. Then he sat on the ground next to Radisson, opposite the Algonquins. Megiscawan filled his pipe deliberately with herbs and tobacco so they could smoke together before talking, in order that their words would travel far and be heard clearly.

Radisson hadn't been in an Indian camp for a long time. It reminded him of how he used to live as an Iroquois. He wasn't afraid. His only handicap was not being able to speak Algonquin well.

The four chiefs were dressed all in leather for the occasion and wore their ceremonial finery: porcupine quill wristbands, leather headbands decorated with drawings of animals and shapes, and furs. Radisson wanted to know what it meant.

The pipe was passed around in a circle. The smoke escaped skyward through a hole in the top of the teepee. Once Megiscawan had set the pipe down on the ground, Godefroy was able to speak, eloquently, in Algonquin.

"Megiscawan and Penikawa know me well. They know I speak with my heart. I offer you these gifts because the Algonquins have been my friends ever since I arrived in your land. The eagle feather signifies that we must rise above the quarrels that divide us. The musket signifies that the French have not abandoned you. Many among us want to help you defeat the Iroquois. I know that the attitude of the grand chief of the Frenchmen—our governor—and the Jesuits disappoints you. I have come to reassure you of our intentions and to listen to you. Speak to me frankly, Megiscawan."

The previous day, Godefroy had explained to Radisson how he planned to go about things. Even though he didn't understand every word, Radisson knew that the captain wanted to focus on reconciliation.

"I thank you for bringing me these gifts," Megiscawan replied. "But I find them difficult to interpret. You want to look beyond our quarrels and yet it is the Frenchmen who have betrayed our alliance by excluding us from the peace with the Iroquois. They have allied with our enemies and abandoned us. Penikawa returned from Trois-Rivières with his hands empty. The Blackrobes did not want to give him the powder he asked for. And yet here you are giving us powder without asking for furs in exchange. Who speaks for the Frenchmen? You or the Blackrobes? Whom must I believe?"

Radisson could tell from Megiscawan's tone and stiff posture that he was not amused.

"I understand that the Algonquins do not know who to believe. I understand your concern," Godefroy replied. "But many Frenchmen are just as concerned as you are. The Jesuits and our grand chief agreed to a separate peace only so that we could get our strength back. Make no mistake, Megiscawan: we have not broken our bond with the Algonquins. We have only bent a little, like bulrushes in a storm. Once the storm has passed, we will stand tall again. Soon the French will impose their will on the Iroquois and our alliance with the Algonquins will be just as strong as before."

Megiscawan nodded to show his appreciation. His silence indicated he was keen to hear more.

"I propose you come meet me this spring at the foot of the great waterfall. I will give you more muskets and ammunition in exchange for your furs. I want you to avoid the same fate as the Hurons. Your bows and arrows will not stand up to the heavy fire of the Iroquois. You need muskets. The feather is to ask you to rise high enough to look back toward the past and forward into the future: we were once allies and allies we will be once again. If you accept my offer and meet us at the waterfall, you will have to be discreet, though: the Iroquois must not find out. Now is not the time to provoke them."

Radisson could see the traces of distrust start to fade away from the faces of the three men. Only Wakopi, the lone woman in the group, still appeared unmoved.

"Before the white men arrived," she said, "nations would come exchange corn, stones, and shells with us. We would give them meat, canoes, and healing plants in return. The Iroquois did not bring their war up here. Then the French arrived and offered us objects that we liked. We became allies. But today, war, disease, and betrayal are ruining everything. Why so much suffering? Why are the French not honest with us? Why are they at war one day and at peace the next with Iroquois?"

"The French are also going through difficult times," Godefroy replied. "Several of our allies have fled and left us alone. We have also been abandoned. I understand the pain felt by my Algonquin brothers, but the French are suffering just as much. We are divided over what should be done to improve our lot. I am holding out my hand to you. Other Frenchmen have taken the hand held out by the Iroquois. Perhaps in the future we will all be reunited. In the meantime, I for one will also remain faithful to my Algonquin friends."

Megiscawan, Penikawa, Kitsikano, and Wakopi exchanged words quietly among themselves. They appeared hesitant.

"We cannot accept or refuse your gifts right away," Megiscawan concluded. "First, we must consult the heads of family. It will take time to gather enough beaver pelts in exchange for the muskets and powder you speak of. All will have to be involved. We must first discuss the matter among ourselves. We will let you know what we decide before winter."

"I look forward to it," Godefroy replied, disappointed. "Before we go, I have a favour to ask. I must return quickly to Trois-Rivières if I am to keep our meeting a secret. I am supposed to be out hunting and I must bring back some game. If you would like to come hunting with Radisson and me you would be doing us a great service."

Megiscawan, Penikawa, and two members of their family agreed to go with them. Three to a canoe, they descended the river with the current, reaching the great waterfall in only three days. There they stopped to hunt.

Penikawa knew better than anyone how to coax the animal spirits and win their favour. That evening, around the fire, Radisson watched as he took a stag's shoulder blade out of a leather bag decorated with porcupine quills and examined it. The Algonquin held it up to the flames, looking for the lines that would show where the game was to be found.

The ritual lasted for a long time and reminded Radisson of the techniques employed by his brother Ganaha. He had forgotten how the Indians would get ready for a hunt by asking the spirits for help. Once the ritual was over, Penikawa put the bone away, looking neither disappointed nor satisfied. Radisson didn't know what to make of it, but vowed to team up with him the next day to measure his talents against the soothsayer's.

The group split into three at sunrise. The two youngest Algonquins went off by themselves. Godefroy went with Megiscawan, and Radisson followed Penikawa, who seemed to know exactly where he was headed. After hiking for over an hour, he stopped to rub his body with balsam boughs and motioned for Radisson to do the same. Now their smell wouldn't chase the wild game away. They set off again more slowly, still under the cover of the evergreen forest, still in silence. Penikawa found and examined a track, then poked at it with his fingers.

"That way. Close," he whispered to Radisson.

The sound of running water told them they were nearing a small creek. It masked the sound of their footsteps and the noise made by the branches they brushed against. Penikawa stood still for a moment. He pushed back the last curtain of foliage that separated them from the river and in one movement took an arrow from his quiver, held up his bow, and fired at a deer that Radisson now saw for the first time, standing on the other shore. The animal reared its head nervously, but it was too late: the arrow had already sliced through its neck. Radisson took aim and fired off a musket shot himself. The deer disappeared into the vegetation.

They hurried across the river and discovered their prey, dead and just steps from the water. Radisson's musket shot had got it square in the chest. The animal had survived its double wound for no more than a few seconds. Penikawa sliced off one of its ears and offered it in silence to the spirit of the deer, which had allowed them to kill this beautiful doe. Radisson looked on in silence, with mixed feelings. He had mostly lost faith in the spirits venerated by the Indians. The constant admonishments of the Jesuits had brought him back to the Christian side ("Thou shalt have no other gods before me."). But the more he thought about it, the more intrigued he was by how Penikawa had walked straight there, without a doubt, without the slightest detour, as though he had known in advance where the deer would be. His strange divining technique appeared to have worked...

At Godefroy's request, they beached their game-laden canoe on a small stretch of sand not far from Trois-Rivières.

"I have something else to ask you," Godefroy told Radisson. "I know that Ragueneau holds you in the highest esteem. He trusts you. Perhaps he will tell you a thing or two he is no longer willing to share with me. If something important comes up, please let me know."

Things were starting to get complicated. Radisson wanted to try to remain on the fence, to serve both the Jesuits and the captain faithfully, while waiting to find out which side was right. But it wouldn't be easy.

"I'm not asking you to betray his confidence," Godefroy went on, seeing Radisson hesitate. "I know Ragueneau. I know his heart's in the right place. All I'm asking is that you put the colony's interests before the Jesuits'. You're smart enough to be able to figure things out for yourself."

"I'll try," Radisson replied.

For the last part of the trip, Godefroy let Radisson steer the canoe. It was an honour: it wasn't every day that the captain of the militia gave up his rightful place in the stern to a young apprentice. When they arrived back in Trois-Rivières, this piece of news spread quickly. Many would never see the young Jesuit charge in the same light again.

November took hold of the village. The harvests were taken in, animals were butchered, the time for long journeys was now over. The first snow covered the ground. It had been a long time since peace and abundance had left those living in the village feeling so serene. But Radisson found that time passed slowly, with nothing to do but chores for the Jesuits.

Father Ragueneau had plenty of time to think. He wondered about the signs God was sending him. He had failed with the Hurons. He had lost his post as superior in Québec. He had just missed his chance to leave for Iroquois country. Perhaps it was time to change how he handled himself. When Radisson returned from the forge where he occasionally went to amuse himself, Ragueneau made an effort not to ask about the latest gossip he might have heard there. He no longer asked after

Marguerite's news when Radisson visited her either. Instead, he contented himself with his work as a pastor, looking after his flock and reminding himself day after day not to be over-zealous. Even with the sour-tempered Iroquois, he vowed to be more tolerant than he had been with the Hurons. He thought about this each time Radisson gave him a lesson in the Iroquois language, in which he was coming on by leaps and bounds.

The smith Charles Aubuchon was always busy with some-thing. He was never in any rush as he went about fashioning axes, latches, hinges, nails, and pikes. Sometimes, he would tackle more ambitious projects like plowshares, and he also enjoyed forging blades for planing mouldings. His forge was the liveliest place in the village. It was always warm there, and the men liked to gather to chat in small groups and smoke their pipes. Some drank more eau-de-vie than was wise. Conversation often turned to the lack of women. The older men would tell how they would travel to distant lands before the war with the Iroquois. These *coureurs des bois* would trade goods and take up with young Indian girls not yet married, in keeping with their traditions. Many of them were all too keen to sleep with a Frenchman—it made them feel exotic and they were grateful for the trinkets the men gave them, too.

Every time he went to the forge, Radisson would hear plenty of malicious gossip: about men who had built their homes poorly, about men who were easily scared, about men who couldn't hunt, about men who had no staying power. The fact there was plenty to eat was a favourite topic of conversation this year. Talking about food seemed to satisfy appetites as much as eating it. It had been a long time since providence had been so good to them.

Radisson was bored. Fortunately, there were the Iroquois language classes to remind him of fond memories and prepare for his return among the Iroquois. He felt reassured that the French had set up home there in large numbers, and that there were true advocates for peace among the Onondaga. He was no longer afraid of being among them.

Now and again, he visited Marguerite. She was also sorry there were not more women in the village. It would have made her life much easier. To be on the safe side, she always keep a poker by the door and only let married men into her home, along with her brother Pierre, the Jesuits, Claude Volant, who was courting her sister Françoise, and neighbour Dandonneau dit Lajeunesse, whom she was careful not to bring in too often before he got any ideas. Médard Chouart was the man for her. She was sure he would come back from his trip alive. She just knew it. And she would love it if Claude Volant married her sister. She knew him well and he was her late husband's best friend.

Her eldest boy had just turned five and was already helping around the house. She was so proud of him. Other women sometimes dropped by to visit... her sister, the carpenter's wife, Jeanne Godefroy, Antoinette Côté. They had fun together and helped each other out. They were good times.

A number of men were buzzing around Françoise. She had no choice but to get married; there were too few women in Trois-Rivières. The kindest suitors brought her food: a fish, a piece of meat, vegetables. They said it was for the Jesuits, but it was only a pretext to get close to Françoise. Others arrived, their hands empty, and behaved like parasites. They told her she was so beautiful, the kitchen smelled so good, the house was so clean and tidy. The most insistent made her feel uncomfortable. When she kept her distance, they came up to her. When she was minding her own business, there they were, under her feet. She sometimes asked Radisson to get them to leave. "Goodnight," he told them, time and again. "See you tomorrow. Time for bed." When the softly-softly approach didn't work, he flat out told them to leave his sister alone. Sparks flew.

Françoise knew which men she did not want to marry. That was easy. But her heart couldn't decide between the two or three she found to her liking. She had trouble choosing one because it was for life. Father Ragueneau had warned her: if she didn't make her mind up soon, he would choose for her, just like any father would. Because he had just about had enough of the men who came to send their imaginations racing over her. They were a source of sin.

Claude Volant had put his role as an officer of the militia on the back burner for the winter. Finding a wife was not to be taken lightly and he intended to give the matter his full attention. He was a fine hunter and could give Françoise a skinned hare or a plucked partridge almost every day. He had also given her a brand new knife from his supply of trading goods. After making sure Françoise was in no doubt as to his intentions, he was wise enough to have a word with Ragueneau or Radisson.

People called him Saint Claude because no one could really find fault with him. His feelings for Françoise were sincere. More than just pretty and hard-working, she was made for this country, a real Radisson, just like Marguerite and Pierre. He was sure she would make the best wife in the world. Ragueneau knew that Claude was a gentleman who wanted to make her happy. He was also Radisson's preferred suitor.

Christmas was coming. Ragueneau visited every household to remind them of the importance of Christ's birth. He wanted one and all to purify their hearts during Advent.

Today was the Godefroys' turn.

Radisson, who went with the priest, hadn't set foot in the house since his capture by the Iroquois. It felt strange to walk through the door again. Pierre Godefroy welcomed him warmly, like a member of the family, but the greeting did not make up for Radisson's memories of François. It was a wound he had trouble healing.

Jeanne, Pierre Godefroy's wife, bustled around, clearing the hearth for the Jesuit. It was quite the visit. She unfolded two trestles stored against the wall and set the table on them. She brought over some salt pork, bread, and water. Her husband, Ragueneau, and Radisson sat facing the fire on simple wooden benches at the end of the long table.

While the Jesuit exchanged news with his host, Radisson looked around the home he had been in so often in the past. He didn't remember the house being so small and cluttered. Four boys and two girls were still living there with their parents. Right next to him, Anne, the family's eldest daughter, caught his attention. She had changed a lot. She was almost a woman now. She was helping her mother prepare a big stew, which was bubbling away over the hearth, in a heavy iron pot hanging from a wooden beam. Smiling and confident, she listened in on the conversation between her father and the Jesuit, often turning toward them.

Radisson was won over by a pretty face and long locks of hair that poked out from under her bonnet, by merry eyes that gleamed with the light of the fire. She was almost of marrying age. Radisson had heard she was already promised to the neighbour's eldest son, Urbain Côté. The two families had known each other forever. And since the two youngsters got on so well, marrying them stood to reason. At any rate, for as long as Radisson was in the service of the Jesuits, he wouldn't be allowed to marry.

"Throughout Advent, you must lead by example," Ragueneau was telling the head of the household. "I often see your wife and daughters at the church and I congratulate them. But you, not so often. And your sons, even less."

"We just don't have the time, Father," Godefroy replied. "It's not that we wouldn't like to. The women are right beside the church, but we're out hunting, fishing, on exercises with the militia... You know that Claude, my eldest boy, often delivers mail to Québec. We're doing our best, Father."

"I'm not criticizing you. I'm just telling you what I see, that's all. I would like you to make an effort during Advent. If people see you going to mass during the week, they'll follow. You have a lot of influence, you know. Much more than I do."

"I doubt that, Father. Everybody here admires you so."

Ragueneau looked at him severely.

"Lying is a sin, you know. I know that many hold the mission I organized to the Iroquois against me. And you are first among them. Admit it. I am far from sure they admire me as much as you say. Of course, everyone greets me politely enough. But I know that many have unkind things to say about me behind my back. I'm no fool. I know what they're up to."

"If you want the truth," replied Godefroy, "it's not so much the mission that upsets me as the way we've let our allies down."

"We had no choice."

"It's going to backfire. It's started already..."

"First, we must secure a peace with the Iroquois. That you cannot deny. If not, we're headed for ruin. At least we are at peace."

"For how long, Father? Can you tell me for how long?"

"Pierre, please. Let's discuss this another time. I came to talk to you about the feast of Christmas and the birth of Christ. What would we do without him? I ask you. So, then, will I see you at mass more often? Yes or no?"

"We'll see," Godefroy replied sullenly.

The Jesuit pulled a face and crossed his arms to show his displeasure. Jeanne intervened.

"Would you like some beef stew, Father? It's almost done."

"Thank you. But I have eaten my fill and I am endeavouring to do penance for my sins, as the Holy Mother Church asks of us. You should consider doing likewise."

"We'll go confess," Godefroy replied dryly. "It amounts to the same thing."

"Very well, that's better than nothing. By the sounds of things, you are in need of it."

Radisson was sorry that his master and his adoptive father were at loggerheads with each other. But he did not interfere. He preferred to watch the fair Anne. She was amused at how the pair brought out the worst in each other; this wasn't the first time they had clashed over nothing. Leaning over a broad plank of wood that was attached to the wall by the fireplace, she was nimbly cutting vegetables. Iron pots and utensils hung beside her. That was the women's corner. Women made all the difference to a home, bringing as much comfort, warmth, and light as the fire. Anne seemed so nice, and just as strong as her mother.

Ragueneau was already getting up to leave. He would come back to preach another time. Anne thanked him for his visit and assured him she would be a regular at mass that Advent.

"We girls will be ready," her mother chipped in. "Don't you worry."

"Thank you. Christmas is such a beautiful festival, a time of hope, of life just beginning. And this year I have a surprise for you. It's going to be the best Christmas you have ever had in Trois-Rivières. You have my word!"

Radisson was in no hurry to leave. He took his time saying goodbye to the fair Anne and his heart gave a leap when she returned his smile and looked him square in the eye. As he walked out the door, Godefroy threw him an inquiring glance.

"No news," Radisson whispered to him on the way past.

"Make sure he gets some time off!" Godefroy shouted at Father Ragueneau as he walked away. "He's not a servant, Radisson! He'd better not lose everything he learned with the Iroquois! Once there's enough snow, I'll bring him moose hunting with me!"

III

WINTER IN THE VILLAGE

AFTER CHECKING THAT THE CHURCH DOOR was locked, as his master required of him, Radisson put each of the three wooden statues that had arrived from Québec two months earlier on their respective pedestals. Ragueneau had kept them in reserve to put a little extra sparkle into the Christmas ceremonies. Radisson then spread straw through the temporary stable at the front of the church. It would house a living nativity scene, just like they had in France.

The Jesuit would have liked to keep the whole thing a secret right to the end, but he wasn't able to set everything up quickly enough. His parishioners had discovered the half-built stable and the empty pedestals a few days earlier. Now he was happy: the rumour had spread around the village that a special midnight mass was being planned and everyone was looking forward to taking part.

Ragueneau came by to see how the work was progressing.

"It's missing a little sparkle, don't you think? The birth of Christ should really shine forth for all to see! What do you say we put all the candles we can find in the chancel?"

"Good idea."

"What could we put on the stable roof? The Bible tells us there were angels playing the trumpet."

Radisson thought for a moment. He didn't see how he was going to come up with angels or trumpets.

"We could add balsam boughs," he suggested, "like we put in our shelters. People are used to that. It would make it homely."

Ragueneau wasn't taken by the idea.

"Hmmm. We don't have much choice, so go ahead and add the balsam boughs. But hurry: I still have an important task for you, a secret for you to keep. See me in my office when you have finished."

The church was full to bursting. The three statues, the decorated stable, and the fifty or so candles had the desired effect. The *habitants* were dazzled by the spectacle and prayed devoutly. Charles Aubuchon, Jeanne Godefroy, and Guillaume Côté sang a hymn. Françoise and Claude walked down the central aisle and took their place in the stable as Mary and Joseph. Who better to embody the hope of a better future? Françoise was moved. Her fiancé was honoured.

Radisson hid in the sacristy until the sermon, as Ragueneau had asked him to, eager to pull off something really special. He held the precious object he was to carry tight against him, surprised by how realistic it looked. He kept an eye on the priest through the doorway.

"What could be more extraordinary than the birth of a child?" Ragueneau asked, beginning his sermon. "A family needs a child to go and help with its share of the work. A child provides assurance that the family line will go on. A child provides security to its parents once their hard work is done.

"But when this child is our living God made man, when it's Jesus Christ our Lord come to save us and atone for our sins, then our joy has no end! Little baby Jesus, so fragile today, so dependent on his parents—represented here by our dear Claude and Françoise, who are getting married in a few days' time—this baby Jesus is the greatest gift that God could give us.

"The Lord, who inspires us all, will be our reward at the hour of our death, when he welcomes those among us who have earned it into the kingdom of heaven. Let us rejoice, my brothers! For at this very moment, Jesus is among us."

That was the signal! Radisson rushed out to Ragueneau and handed him a precious object wrapped in a blanket for the priest to reveal to the congregation: an incredibly lifelike little baby Jesus made of wax. The priest held it out and looked down at it. The congregation gasped as one in surprise and admiration. Slowly, the Jesuit walked around the church, showing off the newborn. Radisson followed his every step, holding candles to light the baby.

"Come admire the Saviour born to us," Ragueneau repeated. "Let us rejoice."

The women blessed themselves. Some were crying. The doll was like a real little baby: clean, smiling, free of pain. The men were also moved. Ragueneau walked through the congregation so that everyone could see for themselves.

"Admire him," he kept repeating. "Adore the God made man to save you."

He at last set the baby down in the cradle in the stable, beside Françoise and Claude, who were feeling overwhelmed in their role as the holy parents. Françoise was crying. Claude didn't know what to do to console her. As the priest performed the rite of transubstantiation, the congregation gathered their thoughts. Rarely had the ritual seemed so real to Ragueneau.

When the time came for communion, he really felt as though he were giving the body and blood of Christ to each person. His soul soared still further when Charles Aubuchon sang a French hymn in his fine deep voice:

Dans cette étable
Que Jésus est charmant
Qu'il est aimable
Dans son abaissement...

In this stable
How delightful Jesus is
How lovely
In his humbling...

The congregation sang along with the chorus enthusiastically. What a beautiful mass! It was one he would remember for a long time. Opposite the altar, Ragueneau put away the hosts, thanking God for having inspired the ceremony. He could feel divine mercy coming down on his suffering and the suffering of the community. It heartened him. Radisson was moved, too.

Ending the mass, Father Ragueneau asked everyone to pray for his friend Le Moyne and all the other Frenchmen celebrating Christmas at the same moment with the Iroquois. In his heart of hearts, he implored the heavens for a lasting peace and hoped he would be able to join them.

The people of Trois-Rivières celebrated New Year's Day exuberantly, following years of dire poverty. They drank to the New Year with hope in their hearts. God willing, a new dawn

had come at last! Many were even prepared to put their dis-
content with the Jesuits behind them after the wonderful
Christmas that Ragueneau had given them. They wanted to
believe the mission would be a success, that things were looking up for the colony. Alcohol flowed like water.

The celebrations were little more than a dress rehearsal for
all those getting ready to mark the wedding of Claude and
Françoise. Despite the inevitable petty jealousies, people were
happy to see them together. It was commonly thought that
Saint Claude, the lucky man, was fully deserving of his
Françoise.

On the morning of the wedding, the betrothed was no longer
sure of her decision.

"It's too late to change your mind now," Marguerite told her
as she helped her get ready. "Claude will make a good husband.
Don't worry. I know him. You couldn't have found a better
man."

Françoise couldn't help but worry her life might suddenly
take a turn for the worse.

"Dry those tears! It's not worth crying over. You need to
take a man in hand. As soon as he's good to you and he's as
happy as can be, you can be happy. They don't call him Saint
Claude for nothing! He's a good man. He has a good head on
his shoulders and he hardly ever drinks. That's important: the
less he bends his elbow, the happier you'll be."

"Maybe I should've gone with Aubuchon. He would have
stayed home with me the whole time. Claude's going to be out
in the bush. I'll worry about him."

"That's where you're wrong, sister of mine. It's not going to
take long for you to realize just how much of a nuisance a man

can be. When he leaves, you'll have peace and quiet. You'll be in charge. No one bothering you or telling you what to do. And when he comes back, you'll be glad to see him. It's for the best."

"You didn't love Véron? You didn't want him to stay home with you?"

"I loved everything about him. He worked hard, he was helpful, good to me. It hurt a lot when he died. But I was still happy for him to go away now and then—and happier still when he came back! A husband who's not always hanging about the house is just perfect. And it helps in bed too, believe me."

Françoise looked away. Talking about sex made her uncomfortable. She wasn't in as much of a rush as other women she knew to sleep with a man. She had spent so long in the church, with her mother, with the nuns...

"That's why you chose another *coureur des bois*?"

"There's not a man as brave as Médard Chouart," replied Marguerite, standing up. "And that's the way I like it. I don't want to lose my second husband. We get attached to them, you know! Médard might be reckless sometimes, but I know he's going to come back."

Françoise felt her strength return.

Radisson couldn't bring himself to be happy. He had even been irritated by Ragueneau, who wouldn't stop going on about how glad he was to be celebrating Claude and Françoise's marriage, sharing in the hope it brought to the community, with everyone looking forward to the patter of tiny feet. Radisson should have refused to be a witness. That way he wouldn't have had a front-row seat to something he couldn't have for himself.

As soon as the ceremony was over, he went outside into the freezing air. He vowed to at least celebrate as much as he liked, no matter what Ragueneau might think. There was only so much he could take of being a good boy.

The happy couple had the honour of being received by Pierre Godefroy as they went into Claude Volant's home, where the wedding banquet was to be held. The chests and table had been put away, but there were so many guests they had to be pushed right to the back of the house. The only two chairs were for the newlyweds. They sat by the fireplace in the small area where Marguerite and Jeanne Godefroy were preparing the first wedding meal, perspiring heavily under their bonnets, heavy dresses, and long aprons.

Since Françoise had no dowry and Claude was his favourite officer of the militia, Pierre Godefroy had a gift for them: a fox fur blanket—said to be the warmest there was—for their bed. Guests had also brought along crockery and made food for the banquet.

Portions of pork stew began to be handed around the lively crowd. Plenty of bread followed, freshly baked that morning, white and tender. Everyone tore off a hunk before passing the loaf on to the next person. Guests raised cups and pitchers of eau-de-vie above their heads to wish happiness and many children to the married couple. Radisson had rarely seen so much elation concentrated in such a small space. People were still careful not to drink too much, though, since Ragueneau was expected from one minute to the next.

When the Jesuit arrived, Claude Volant gave him his chair. He was served a portion of stew and several guests came over to greet him. He had trouble eating there were so many polite remarks to be exchanged. Ragueneau then gave the couple some good Christian advice and again wished them much happiness and many children, sincerely because he was very fond of both.

Since he felt a little like a father to Françoise, next he unwrapped the gift he had brought in lieu of a dowry: a wooden crucifix to hang above the front door, prunes from France straight out of his personal stash, and three *écus*.

"Your father would have given much more, of that I am quite certain, but I cannot take his place and these three *écus*, which I have blessed, are like the Holy Trinity. They will bring you both luck and protect you."

Ragueneau did not linger long, because it was not done for a priest to attend a wedding banquet. There would be excesses that he preferred to have no knowledge of, a diabolical, contagious madness he could already feel in the air, which, fortunately, would last no more than a few days. Opposing it would be futile, even dangerous to his authority. And he knew it. On his way out, he gave Françoise a kiss as the men protested, at last given an opportunity to poke fun at him for his relationship with his attractive housekeeper without committing the sin of spreading malicious gossip. He slipped out after embracing Claude.

As soon as the priest had left the house, the guests whooped with joy. The party was well and truly underway. Claude Volant passed around more pitchers of eau-de-vie in all directions. He took Françoise by the waist and twirled her around, bumping into those around them. In the twinkling of an eye, thirty people were up dancing, the floor sagging dangerously beneath their feet. God only knew how so many guests managed to wriggle around in such a small space with no one being crushed. The others beat time, shouting out and clapping their hands. Claude's cousin Mathurin Volant, singing at the top of his lungs beside the front door, could barely be heard. He intended to stick close to the door all night to make sure no jealous men tried to spoil the party or, worse, put a jinx on the married couple.

People sang back and forth. Dancers came and went on the dance floor. Radisson let himself get caught up in the jubilation and swayed to the music. He spotted Françoise among the dancers and thought he had never seen her looking so happy. Marguerite and Jeanne Godefroy cooked on with another housewife who had just arrived. The women had stirred up the fire, which was now roaring with light and warmth. It was like being in an overheated house in the middle of summer. Mathurin opened the door to let some of the heat out. A handful of men went outside to drink. Mathurin kept an eye on the comings and goings without touching a drop of alcohol. Radisson meanwhile gave in to a few fiery sips of eau-de-vie.

As soon as Marguerite stepped away from the hearth to get some fresh air, three men swarmed around her.

"You're a fool to wait for Médard," one of them said. "He's not coming back! I'd make a much better husband."

"Leave me alone!" she retorted.

"All you have to do is say yes," another added. "I'll give you everything I own. Say yes, Marguerite. You're never going to see Médard again."

"Clear out!"

The third brazenly pinched her butt.

"Keep your paws off!" she cried, shoving him back.

Already drunk, the man grabbed Marguerite by the shoulder to keep his balance.

"Been a while since you've had a man between your thighs, I'd say. Go on, you know you want it."

"Don't you touch me, you drunk!" she said again, shoving him harder this time. "Not if you were the last man in Hell..."

The man fell over, dropping his cup. Marguerite grabbed the poker and brandished it at all three of them.

"The next man to say Médard isn't coming back and I'll make mincemeat out of him!"

Radisson had seen the altercation and edged his way across the room.

"Everything all right, Sis?"

"Don't worry, Pierre. I know how to stick up for myself. But if you like, you can throw that one outside. I'm sick of the sight of him!"

Big Latouche tried to sneak away, but he had trouble picking himself up. Radisson grabbed him by the collar and dragged him to the door. The other two admirers slipped off without having to be asked twice. Radisson let off some steam on the drunk, who was trying to wriggle free. He gave him a shake.

"Open the door so he can get some air," he said to Mathurin.

Then he threw him as hard as he could out into the snow.

"Don't let me catch you sniffing around my sister again. Otherwise you'll have me to deal with!"

He turned to Mathurin:

"Don't let him back in. The party's over for him."

"You can count on it. You won't see him inside again."

Back in the house, Radisson noticed Anne Godefroy had joined the three women to serve the next meal. How had she gotten in? He hadn't seen her come in. But she looked amazing! That much was clear. She attracted him, like magnetic north pulls the needle on a compass. He wanted to go up and speak to her, but he wasn't too sure how to go about it.

Why not help the women hand out the food? He picked up bowls and plates and piled them by the hearth. Once they were full, he passed them around, going back and forth to the fireplace. Each time he got close to Anne, his desire for her increased. He almost dropped a pile of plates when she grabbed him by the shoulder and shouted "Watch out!" to make sure a clumsy oaf didn't bump into him. His chest was on fire. She was so strong, responsible, industrious, full of life, cheerful, good-looking, kind... A couple of times, he saw young Côté, her betrothed, who had no more to offer the fair Anne than he had. Far from it. If he hadn't undertaken to serve the Jesuits, he might have stood a chance. He was going to try his luck anyway. He took a big gulp of eau-de-vie, which left him dizzy.

Trying hard to think about something else, he moved well away from the fire and ate his portion of goose stew and vegetables. The flavours exploded in his mouth. It was absolutely delicious! He couldn't remember the last time he had eaten so well. He licked his plate clean. Hurrah for the women who made men so happy! How lucky were the fortunate few who found one for life! Try as he might, he couldn't turn his thoughts away from the fair Anne. Some revellers had already put down their plates. People were shouting, singing, drinking, making a fuss everywhere he looked. Anne didn't seem to be intimidated by the racket and remained as appealing as the prospect of heaven when his days were done. "Never mind," thought Radisson. "It's a wedding day and everyone is a mess. Maybe there's hope for me yet."

He went back to the hearth, where Marguerite caught him on the way by.

"Still hungry? Here, have the rest of this. You won't have a feast like this every day."

It was really and truly delicious. Radisson savoured every bite as he stared at Anne, who was over by the hearth. She didn't see him. Before he had a chance to speak to her, Marguerite came looking for him.

"Go gather the plates, would you? Take everything you can. And don't break anything!"

Radisson had trouble making his way through the crowd. The revellers were back up dancing. Charles Aubuchon's loud singing could still be heard over the din. Those too drunk to dance clapped their hands half-heartedly. Once Radisson had gathered the plates, he noticed, much to his dismay, that Anne had disappeared. Her parents, too. They had left to make sure their marriageable daughter got to bed safely. Some more eau-de-vie for Radisson...

Claude Volant kept singing at the top of his lungs, still very sober for a groom on his wedding night. Françoise sang along with him heartily, a glint in her eye and a smile almost always on her lips. Radisson hadn't thought she was capable of so much enthusiasm. She was happy. It was there for all to see. He had seen her take a few sips of eau-de-vie, but it was the wedding that had made her so happy. Claude was so delighted that she had chosen him from among so many single men that he showered her with attention. He was quite the gentleman. Françoise felt appreciated and reassured. She had understood she was his little treasure, his promise of happiness, the key to his family and lineage. She had opened the doors to her husband's future for him. She couldn't wait to be with him for good and to begin her new life.

The jokes got ruder as the night progressed. Soon the happy couple would slip off to cousin Mathurin's home for their first night together as lovers. A few revellers went back home to rest for a few hours, but most would stay and party all night. Claude and Françoise made the most of the comings and goings to sneak out. Mathurin walked them back to his house and when he returned he called for a glass and drank to their happiness. Again and again to catch up with the other drinkers. Radisson was still drinking. He was swept away by the singing and dancing until the middle of the night, when the alcohol brought him down. He fell exhausted to the floor, near the fire that the hardier revellers were keeping going, and slept soundly for an hour or two.

When he woke up in the small hours of the morning, a dozen or so people were gathered around the fire, telling each other legends and tales of the supernatural, their eyes red with tiredness, their faces puffed up with alcohol. Radisson went outside for a moment to recover his senses in the ice-cold air under the first rays of sunshine. Minutes later, Claude and Françoise came back in to keep the party going, to the great delight of the guests. Radisson was struck by how happy they looked.

"Oh! Oh!" Bailly the carpenter, who still hadn't slept, shouted over. "I see those little Indian girls showed you how it's done, Claude. Just look how happy that wife of yours looks now!"

Françoise looked at the floor. She blushed a little. Trying to appear composed, she took the table, which had been put away along the wall, and put it up on its trestles. She began making pancake mix for breakfast. Claude brought her eggs. Simone Bailly, who had also stayed up all night, wiped down the plates. Claude took a sip of eau de vie to get back into the swing of things and started singing. Françoise threw a handful of dry branches onto the crackling fire. She started making pancakes in a pan. Guests who had been dozing came up to the fire for a bite to eat, more to shake off their tiredness than to satisfy any hunger. Radisson ate, too, unsettled by the alcohol and by how happy the newlyweds were.

Anne Godefroy came back, which almost knocked him off his feet. She really was too good-looking, too full of life, too attractive, and he was too much of a fool to have given his word to the Jesuits... He would give everything he had to hold her in his arms. He would marry her right there and then! But she wasn't his to ask. It was impossible. He took another slug of eau-de-vie and moved off to the back of the house.

Marguerite came back at that moment and asked for someone to help her bring in the piece of frozen venison she wanted to roast for that night's supper. Radisson stayed back. Other guests added to the numbers. Soon there would be as many people as there had been the previous day. The singing and dancing picked up again, interrupted by food, stories, and eau-de-vie. Radisson spent the day in an alcohol-induced daze, bitter while pretending to be enthusiastic, until he fell once again into a sound night's sleep.

|||||||||||||||||||||||||||||||||||||||||||||||||||||||||||||||||||||||||||||||||||||||||||||||||

CHAPTER 8

COLD SWEAT

R ADISSON WAS JUST ABOUT FINISHED TIDYING the
church—what a bore—when Father Ragueneau cried out
from afar. He sounded anxious.

"Radisson! Radisson! Come quickly!"

Radisson rushed to the residence, shouting, "What's
happened?"

"A group of Iroquois ambassadors! Something must be
wrong for them to come in the middle of winter like this."

Radisson met him at the door.

"You're sure, Father?"

"What do you take me for? An idiot? I know an Iroquois
when I see one! They say they have come to talk, but I don't
know. Quick, follow me."

"It's hard to believe!"

"Worrying, you mean. It's very worrying."

Once he had gotten over his astonishment, the guard at the
main gate to the fort of Trois-Rivières had ushered the four
unarmed Iroquois inside. As he understood it, they had come
with a message for the Jesuits. Father Ragueneau had asked
them to wait before the kitchen fireplace while he fetched
Radisson, who knew the Iroquois language very well. A gut

feeling had put him on the alert immediately. He feared for the fifty Frenchmen who were in Iroquois country.

When Ragueneau and Radisson returned to the kitchen, the Iroquois ambassadors were quietly warming themselves by the fire, dressed in long beaver coats. Radisson was reassured to see them so relaxed. The Jesuit spoke to them in his limited vocabulary.

"Why have you come in the middle of winter? What is so urgent?"

The eldest Iroquois, who seemed to have been most troubled by the cold, walked forward hesitantly. His face was radiant, despite his fatigue.

"We have come to deliver you a message from the Blackrobe who has lived among us for one year now. Here it is. You will no doubt be glad to hear from him. We are here to assure you that our peace and friendship will last for a long time."

Ragueneau took the crumpled parchment from him without even looking at it, his eyes glued to the old chief.

"Once you have read it, we can parley," the chief added. "You should know that many Onondaga were unhappy to see so many Frenchmen arriving, with so many bags. We have come to talk with you about how they can settle in our land in such a way that both peoples are satisfied and peace is maintained."

Radisson picked up on Ragueneau's imperceptible grimace. Unlike the Jesuit, he was not surprised the Iroquois wanted to discuss accommodations, given the difficult negotiations before the French had left the previous summer.

"Why the urgency?" Ragueneau asked. "You could have waited until the spring. Why take such a gruelling trip in winter?"

The old chief caught his breath and glanced at his companions before replying.

"Peace is worth a few frozen toes. The season is favourable to discussion and agreement. In the spring, you will no doubt be preparing a new expedition. In the summer, we will be ready to welcome other Frenchmen among us. We had to come now. But first read the letter from Father Le Moyne. He will explain everything. In the meantime, tell us where we can sleep and get something to eat. Our travels were exhausting. We will need to get our strength back."

Once the Iroquois had been put in the only spare room with a fireplace, the fire had been lit, and straw mattresses had been brought up, Brother Leboeme prepared them a hearty meal. Back in his office, the Jesuit checked with Radisson that he had understood.

"That's right," Radisson confirmed. "He says other Frenchmen will go to their lands next summer. Sounds encouraging."

"I'm not so sure. He also said there were things that had to be negotiated to maintain the peace between us."

"True."

"I don't like the sound of that."

"You know, Father, it's a big step passing from being an enemy to a friend. It seems to me it's normal to still have a few issues to settle."

His eyes trained on the floor, Ragueneau thought hard as he stroked his chin with his long fingers.

"First I'll read what Father Le Moyne has written. Come back tomorrow morning before we meet with them again."

Dear Paul,

How can I express my satisfaction following the arrival of the expedition you prepared? True, we had to negotiate hard to set ourselves up as we wished, for even our friends here did not expect us so soon, or in such numbers. The Iroquois ended up accepting our presence among them. They marked out a spot perfectly suited to our intentions, some distance from their largest village. From here, we are within easy reach of four or five Onondaga villages. We are welcome everywhere we go. At the moment, Father Le Mercier is going around the neighbouring villages with Father Ménard and Father Dablon. He has been gone for several weeks, but messengers assure me all is well. For my part, I regularly preach with Father Frémin in the biggest village in their land, Onondaga. It is very close to here and at least one thousand live there. We are on good terms with our allies, and they are influential.

We have finished building our cabins for the winter. We put up a small enclosure to keep out the animals. We intended to erect a proper palisade, but the Iroquois forbade it. The emissaries who brought you this message will discuss the matter with you.

I am confident they will allow us to build the fort we so desire, which will enable us to establish ourselves here securely. In any event, the Iroquois are more conciliatory than upon our arrival.

The most important thing is that they be open to the word of God. Which is the case. Many among them come to listen to me and ask me questions.

I enclose a list of goods that would be of use to us. You may bring them with you next summer, for the Iroquois have told me they will guide other Frenchmen to where we are. The emissaries to whom I handed over this note told me this before they left. We shall need more munitions and muskets, as much for us as for the Iroquois. Bring more goods, for they would like to trade more. We are already running out.

I would like to share with you in person the hope that grows in my heart each day regarding the rich harvest that awaits us here. The Iroquois are curious, attentive, and perspicacious. There are great minds among them. They can see that our presence in their land is to their advantage.

Do not be worried. We lack for nothing. We cannot complain.

May God help us.

Simon Le Moyne

The meeting between the four emissaries, Father Ragueneau, and Radisson was held in the kitchen the following morning. The two Frenchmen had consulted each other just before. This time, the old chief, very much weakened, remained in the background. The strongest member of the group took over.

"We want the French to repair our muskets," he said. "The Dutch do it for the Mohawk nation and we know the French also repair theirs. We no longer want to trade our furs for new muskets every time they break. You say you do not have many new muskets for us, so we want those we already have to last longer."

The Iroquois stopped talking, arms folded across his chest, back straight as a post. His expressionless face contrasted with the old chief's attitude the previous day. Father Ragueneau turned to Radisson to be sure he understood.

"Is he asking us for more muskets or simply to repair those they already have?"

"He wants us to start repairing all their muskets. But he wouldn't say no if we gave him some more."

"We'll recruit a gunsmith from Québec and bring him with us. That's not difficult. Tell him we agree. But ask him what they will give us in return."

BACK TO THE NEW WORLD

For the first time in a long time, Radisson prepared to speak to an Iroquois. He took a second or two to calm his nerves and thought about which words he wanted to use.

"We will go back with you next summer with a man who repairs muskets," he said. "It is a reasonable request and the French accept. We want to know if that will be enough to allow us to build the fort we desire."

"No," the big man replied. "Repairing our weapons is the first condition. There is also a second."

A third emissary moved forward to speak. His attitude was bordering on the aggressive.

"The Frenchmen arrived among us in great numbers. We welcomed them despite our surprise. Five Blackrobes are now walking around our villages explaining to all that the God of the Frenchmen is the most powerful. We listen to them. But the Frenchmen are behaving like enemies. They want to build a huge palisade around their homes. They say it is for their protection. We asked them to stop acting in this way because they are living among us and we are protecting them. They are our brothers. The Blackrobes and the chief who always wears a sword on his belt responded that it was a tradition of the Frenchmen, wherever they go. We are prepared to accept your traditions. Provided you respect our own."

Radisson watched a wave of concern wash over Father Ragueneau's face.

"We have already adopted many Hurons," the Iroquois went on firmly. "Now they live among us, according to our customs. We want to adopt more."

Ragueneau couldn't help but give a start.

"The Hurons' place is with us. Those who live with the Frenchmen would be happier in our land. We offer them the chance to return to their families, their brothers, their customs. If the French now want peace with the Onondaga, if they want to remain among us for a long time and build this fort, they must bring Hurons with them next summer. That is the second condition."

Ragueneau could barely contain his anger. He looked visibly on edge. Radisson could see him clench his fists. The Jesuit's intuition had not been wrong: this second condition outraged him. The Iroquois emissary was waiting for an answer that did not come. A heavy silence weighed over the six men. None of them moved. At last, Ragueneau recovered his powers of speech. He tried to mutter something noncommittal, his voice scrambled with emotion.

"I cannot give you a reply today. I must first speak to our grand chief, the governor. But I am surprised by your request."

The Jesuit turned to Radisson to ask him to translate his thoughts more exactly.

"Ask him why he wanted to adopt Hurons when his people massacred them by the thousand not even six years ago! Ask him what has changed. Why should we trust them? What guarantee can he give me that his people will not harm the Hurons we bring to them? Ask him that."

Radisson faithfully translated the Jesuit's words, toning down the outrage the Iroquois had surely detected.

"The French and we were at war, but now we are at peace," the Iroquois responded. "The time has come to make peace with the Hurons also. They are our brothers."

"You are your brother's keeper," Ragueneau muttered to himself.

He turned back to Radisson.

"Ask him why they demanded our Indian allies be excluded from the peace. I don't believe him when he says he wants what's best for the Hurons. He's lying. I'm certain of it."

This time Radisson could not translate all Ragueneau had said without causing a deadlock. The Iroquois hesitated all the same before replying to the question, long enough for the fourth emissary to speak in his place. He was the friendliest of the lot. He had remained calm throughout the discussion and Radisson could see kindness in his eyes.

"I understand your surprise," he said in a reassuring tone. "We arrive in your land unexpectedly and speak of a great change in our hearts. I know you were living among the Hurons when we attacked their land. You know that some of them joined with us and that no harm came to them. Today, hundreds of them live among us as brothers. We invite the Hurons who took refuge with the Frenchmen to come join us. The time is coming when we will all be at peace: Frenchmen, Hurons, Iroquois, Algonquins, and all who wish to join us beneath the great tree of peace as foretold by Deganawida."

Deganawida! The name reminded Radisson of the impassioned words of his adoptive father, words that he could hear again and again in his dreams. He also remembered that the great prophet had led many Iroquois warriors to take arms against those who did not respond to their invitation, his father Garagonké first among them. Yes, peace was possible... provided the Iroquois got what they wanted. Radisson nevertheless had faith in this chief. He seemed sincere. Radisson was sure he was a true advocate for peace.

"I understand that you must discuss with other chiefs from your nation before giving us an answer," the Iroquois went on. "But you must understand that we cannot return home with our hands empty. We have made a very long journey to come speak to you frankly. We bring with us the requests of all our nation. The Onondaga want to rekindle our friendship with our Huron brothers and we are waiting for encouraging words from the Frenchmen on this matter. This is the condition upon which the French will still be welcome among us and will be able to settle in our lands according to their traditions."

"Shall I translate for you? Radisson asked Ragueneau.

"No. I understood. Besides, I've heard enough for today."

The Jesuit appeared shaken.

"We will pick up our discussions tomorrow," he declared, turning on his heel.

Radisson followed him out of the room.

The four Iroquois returned to their room, helping their old chief, who could no longer walk alone. Given his worsening condition, Brother Leboeme brought him a warm broth. The Iroquois refused, saying they had all the remedies they needed to cure him.

Once back in his office, Ragueneau asked Radisson to translate every word the last emissary had said.

The Jesuit was not in the least reassured. His face pale and his back hunched, Ragueneau stayed quiet. Radisson had never seen him in such a state.

Ragueneau had not thought the Iroquois would ask for so much. He felt betrayed. He was under no illusions and scarcely believed the last chief's kind words. In his eyes, the Iroquois had not come so far, in the midst of winter, for a simple request. It was a demand. If the French did not comply by transferring a number of Hurons to their lands, peace was in jeopardy and the fifty men in Iroquois country would be in grave danger.

The request was asking enormous sacrifices of Ragueneau. In the middle of the catastrophe that had ruined the Jesuit mission among the Hurons, it was he who had set fire to Sainte-Marie, undoing ten painstaking years of hard work. Along with Father Chaumonot, Ragueneau had saved a few hundred converted Hurons *in extremis*, bringing them to Québec despite the terrible conditions. Had it all been in vain? Had the two missionaries who had been tortured and put to death by the Iroquois sacrificed their lives for naught?

Ragueneau could not decide. The Huron adventure had been exciting, although it had ultimately left a bitter taste in his mouth. Ragueneau couldn't believe it might end in such utter failure. And yet he felt there was no alternative than to promise these Iroquois they would deliver Hurons to their lands, even if that meant later trying to minimize the consequences of this promise.

Throughout this one-way conversation Radisson had simply listened to his master share his darkest thoughts, but Radisson had not lost hope. In his eyes, being on good terms with the Iroquois was still possible. He even thought it entirely possible the Hurons would be adopted and treated well, as had been the case for Radisson and his mother Katari, herself a Huron. Judging by his own experience, it was a very real possibility. And Andoura, the kindly chief, would surely be able to help them.

A final, brief meeting was held the following day. There were now only three Iroquois emissaries. The old chief was so ill he could no longer get out of bed. His companions were eager to leave. Andoura took charge of bringing the negotiations to a close.

"I have thought long and hard," Ragueneau told him in the Iroquois language. "I accept your second condition. I will convince our governor to let me bring Hurons to your land. But I have a condition of my own. You must let the French build their fort before we come to your land next summer. If the Iroquois guides who come fetch us do not bring a message from Father Le Moyne indicating that the fort has been completed, neither I nor a single Huron will set foot on your land. That is my response."

The three emissaries glanced at each other.

"We are satisfied by your offer," Andoura responded. "We will allow the Frenchmen to build their fort before coming for you. We will meet you in Montréal on the longest day. You will see. The Hurons will be treated well. The Frenchmen will not be disappointed."

Radisson gave a start when Andoura theatrically held out an eagle-head knife identical to his own. His first instinct was to check to see if his knife was still where he carried it under his clothes. It was. He couldn't believe it.

"This knife is a guarantee of our peace," Andoura declared, holding it above his head. "It shows the French will always be welcome among the Onondaga. When you come, the paths will be cleared, the hills levelled, the ditches filled, the rivers calmed. You shall encounter no obstacle along the way. May the prophecy of Deganawida be fulfilled and may our sons and daughters still enjoy the peace that has come between us."

Radisson was shocked. How could there be two copies of such a special knife? How could they both bear the same message for peace? Again he heard his sister Conharassan tell him: "Your knife is too beautiful to use for killing... It's not a knife for war." And his father repeat to him: "First look for peace before you fan the flames of war."

Since his return to Trois-Rivières, the energy emanating from the knife had been much weaker. Sometimes Radisson even forgot it was there, along with the power he associated with it. But the sudden appearance of an identical knife knocked him sideways. His emotions got the better of him and he didn't know what to think. He rubbed his eyes to check to see if he was dreaming. But there was no getting around it: there was the same eagle-head handle, the same broad beak, the same sleek feathers as Andoura put it back in the sheath he wore around his waist. Incredible, but true. Radisson took it to be a sign that his Iroquois adventure would be under a lucky star.

"May God bless you," Ragueneau added, making the sign of the cross with his hand. "We will see each other again next summer."

The meeting was over. Ragueneau walked slowly out of the kitchen, overcome by his failure to fend off the setback. Now he would be forced to betray his dear Hurons. He would also have to inform the governor of the terrible news as quickly as possible.

Radisson's heart, on the other hand, was filled with hope after a knowing glance from Andoura.

That night, he had a dream. His adoptive father Garagonké appeared before him. He stood where Andoura had been standing and moved just like him. He said the same things, inviting the French to come to the land of the Onondaga. Then he turned to Radisson, handed him an eagle-head knife and said: "Take this knife, my son, and be brave, for the lives of the Frenchmen are in your hands."

When he woke up, Radisson remembered what had happened, but was not sure what it meant. Hoping to understand, he held his knife. A powerful current of energy ran through his whole body, along with a curious blend of fear and confidence. He didn't know whether to be happy or worried, although he did feel ready to face anything life might throw at him. After a moment, since no feeling stood out in particular and his dream was beginning to fade away, he got up, his thoughts turned to other matters.

A few hours later, the three able-bodied Iroquois emissaries left Trois-Rivières, carrying the ill chief on a sled. They disappeared quickly into the woods.

A lot of snow had fallen over the past few days. Pierre Godefroy deemed the conditions perfect for moose hunting. Radisson jumped at the chance, delighted to take part in a hunt that

neither the French nor the Iroquois had allowed him to be involved in before, saying he was too young.

Two Algonquins who lived near the village, Guillaume Côté, Pierre Dandonneau dit Lajeunesse, and Radisson went with Godefroy, the expedition leader. The six men and their three dogs left on snowshoes on a cold February morning. They went north, each dragging a small sled loaded with gear. They followed the Saint-Maurice river for three days, then headed west into the first hills they met.

As they had hoped, a great deal of snow had accumulated in the steep-sided valley Godefroy had chosen. The valley formed a bend with a broader valley that had a long lake at the back of it. Here, a forest of young leafy trees attracted moose, which fed on their buds over the winter. The men scaled a long slope to the top of the hill overlooking both valleys. They made their camp in among the balsam trees, hidden away and protected from the wind.

Using their snowshoes, the Frenchmen dug a big round hole in the snow while the Algonquins gathered balsam boughs and spread them out at the bottom of the pit. The frame of their cabin was made from long poles forming a star, meeting in the centre and covered in moose skins they had brought with them. They then covered the sides of their shelter with a thick layer of snow. In a few hours, it was ready. Just beside the entrance—which was well sheltered from the wind—they lit a large fire and kept it burning permanently. Thanks to the narrow opening they had made in the roof opposite the door, heat circulated from the entrance to the back of the shelter. Wool blankets and a few beaver pelts kept them nice and warm.

Radisson loved his first complete immersion in winter. He appreciated both the Indians' ingenuity and the shrewdness of the French for borrowing their customs. Like anyone who knew his way around Canada, he was dressed half like an Indian and half like a Frenchman; he was never cold in his fur and wool clothing. He was delighted to see the sled glide so effortlessly across the snow and by the fact that it was easier to carry the same load in winter than it was in summer. His snowshoes had also saved him a lot of energy. Only the man at the head of the group had trouble walking through the snow; anyone walking behind him had an easy time of it. They regularly swapped places, which meant they could cover long distances without getting tired. Radisson had never seen winter in such a favourable light. He had literally fallen in love with it.

At sunrise the next day, the six men split into three groups to look for moose tracks. Radisson teamed up with Pierre Godefroy. Dandonneau and Côté went off together, and the two Algonquins made up the third duo. Godefroy chose to examine the narrow valley they had come down, while the others walked along the shoreline of the long lake in the other valley. Now that they were alone, Godefroy had a question or two for Radisson.

"Everyone's talking about the visit from the Iroquois," Godefroy said, walking ahead of Radisson. "But no one knows what to think, because Ragueneau won't tell us a thing, as usual. You met them. What do you think?"

"I wanted to speak with you about that. I think it's important. They came to discuss the French settling in their land. Father Ragueneau is very upset."

"Is that so?" said Godefroy, slowing down. "How come? Is the peace under threat already?"

"No, not at all. The Iroquois want to keep the peace with us at any price. They even said they want to include our allies. They brought a message from Father Le Moyne with them. He writes that all is well over there."

They came upon a track that might have belonged to a moose, but Godefroy's thoughts were elsewhere.

"Why did they come in the middle of winter? What was so important?"

"They had conditions."

"What conditions?" Godefroy snapped.

He stopped dead at the edge of a windswept glade and turned to face an uncomfortable Radisson. It was a delicate subject. The young man wanted to faithfully report what had taken place at the meetings so that the captain would be able to act on the information, as agreed. But he was worried about his reaction.

"Let me explain. The four chiefs spoke in turn. I was the interpreter. The first said the Onondaga had been surprised to see fifty Frenchmen arriving at once."

"Of course they were! I always said the Jesuits were in too much of a hurry. You saw it. We had to twist their arm for them to bring our men with them."

"The second chief said they had given the Frenchmen a warm welcome all the same, that they allowed them to settle in their lands. Apart from one thing… They didn't want to let them build the fort they had been planning."

"Why ever not?" asked Godefroy, again surprised.

"They think the French are behaving like enemies in their own land. They warned Ragueneau there were conditions to be met if the French were to settle as they wanted."

"What conditions? Go on, spit it out! What are they?"

Passing over the crests of the hills around them, the sun suddenly shone down on them with all its force. Its light came back up off the snow, and Radisson screwed up his face. He had made it to the most difficult part. Too bad. Out he came with it.

"The Iroquois want us to return to their land next summer with another expedition. But we must bring a gunsmith with us, to repair their muskets… and Hurons, too."

"Jesus!" Godefroy exclaimed, spitting into the snow.

He bit his lip so as not to swear a second time, then spun around and charged straight ahead, mumbling incomprehensibly to himself.

"That's not all," Radisson added as he tried to catch him up. "Another chief—a real advocate for peace, I'm sure of it—says they want to form one people with them, and with us."

Godefroy didn't hear him. Radisson quickly fell behind and preferred to stop.

"And what about the tracks?" Radisson shouted, now far behind. "Didn't we come here looking for moose?"

There was nothing to be done. Godefroy charged on without answering him.

"I'm going anyway," Radisson shouted after him. "I'm going to the Iroquois! My place is there with Father Ragueneau! And we're going to bring the Hurons with us! It's all been settled."

He didn't mention the second eagle-head knife that so inspired confidence in him. That was a matter for him and him alone. At any rate, no one was going to stop him going back to the Iroquois. His destiny lay there.

Once he had at last calmed down, Godefroy stopped. He walked back slowly. His wool coat, kept in place by a broad belt, swayed in the breeze; his long hair peeked out from underneath his woollen tuque. When he got close to Radisson, he looked him in the eyes and began to speak in a calm and controlled voice.

"Later, I'll tell you a few things you don't know. Important things. But for now you should know that, if that's what you want, I encourage you to go to the Onondaga with Ragueneau. You know them better than any of us and you'll be able to see their intentions for what they are. But what you just told me is very serious indeed. We'll talk about it later. In the meantime, let's go back and take another look at that track."

The three groups of hunters each found moose tracks. The Algonquins had even seen a large bullmoose, although he had run off into the woods. The young saplings had been ravaged, however, and it would be more difficult to find the moose again now that they were looking for a new source of food.

They were posted at the foot of the hill where they had made their camp, some three hundred paces away from each other on the line that marked where the conifers ended and the deciduous forest began. All day long, they scanned an area that ran from the long lake to the spot where Godefroy and Radisson had found a track. A good-looking bull dropped by, but one of the three dogs started barking right away and the moose ran for cover in the balsam trees. No one fired for fear of scaring away other moose nearby. That evening, the dog that had cost them was scolded and given nothing to eat while the hunters sought comfort in the shelter after a testing day spent standing around in the cold. In the damp half-light, as the fire roared and crackled by the entrance, Godefroy revised their strategy.

At dawn the next morning, the men stationed themselves in twos around a huge triangle, each pair with a dog. The first two duos hid on either side of the tip of the lake, where the moose had appeared the day before. If a moose were to show up again, their job was to drive it toward the deep valley where Godefroy and Radisson were posted. It would be at its most vulnerable in this narrow passage.

But no moose came by that day.

They applied the same strategy the next day. As a precaution, the two Algonquins had brought enough provisions with them to follow a wounded animal for two or three days. Clouds masked the sun. The cold was damp and bitter. They needed all their endurance to remain in position for hours at a time. But their patience was rewarded when a magnificent moose around ten years old appeared at the tip of the lake.

The animal walked unsuspectingly towards the steep-sided valley. The three dogs didn't make a sound. The first two pairs let the animal pass; it was beyond the range of their muskets in any case. When the moose was far beyond Dandonneau's and Côté's position, the pair jumped out of their hiding place and made as much noise as they could. Their dog attacked, barking with all its strength and leaping around in the snow. Wearing their snowshoes, Côté and Dandonneau ran one after the other towards the moose, which quickened its pace. It was heading towards Godefroy and Radisson. Its long legs sank down deep into the snow. The Algonquins, too far removed from the action, lay in wait.

The shouts of the men and the yaps of the dog, which was making ground on the moose, frightened the animal. It struggled to run away, but ran out of breath quickly. Godefroy and Radisson remained in their hiding place, carefully watching as their prey approached, when the animal broke away towards the hill opposite and began to make its way up the slope to hide in the stand of balsam trees. Radisson and Godefroy dashed out to give chase, too. There was no time to lose. The moose plunged into the snow up to its chest. It sank down in and freed itself, started off again, then sank back down. The protection offered by the balsam trees was getting closer. Godefroy took a chance and fired a shot from a distance, wounding the panic-stricken animal, which continued on its way with the energy born of despair. A trail of blood splashed across the sparkling snow. Godefroy's and Dandonneau's dogs met and began running twice as hard to reach their prey.

The moose turned around to face the dogs. Radisson had trouble following the captain; he had surprising stamina.

Radisson stopped to fire off a shot of his own, also from afar, while Godefroy reloaded his musket. He rushed his shot and missed the target. The noise startled the moose and it turned around and again tried to flee to the top of the hill. But its strength was deserting it. The snow was too deep, the hill too steep. It chose to come back down the hill and charged at the dogs. It tried to strike them with its front legs. Godefroy ran up with his reloaded musket. He stopped and fired a second time. The moose, struck in the chest, fell to its knees, but picked itself up again and butted the dog as it tried to bite its neck. The king of the woods snorted feebly amid the furious barking. Radisson came from not far away and aimed carefully. He shot, this time hitting the animal in the head. The moose collapsed in a heap. Lying in the snow, it did not move again.

Godefroy was the first to reach the dying animal. He ordered the dogs back. Radisson joined him, his heart pounding, amazed at the courageous animal's power. Even in death, it was magnificent! Their strategy had paid off; they had finally gotten the better of it. The hunters had reason to be proud of themselves. Thanks to them, ten or fifteen people would be eating meat for several weeks.

Côté and Dandonneau arrived shortly afterwards, out of breath. They had heard the Algonquins fire two shots while they were running over. Perhaps they had killed another moose. Godefroy barely heard them, too busy with his long knife dismembering the still-quivering animal. The day was drawing to a close. There was no time to lose if they wanted to bring the moose back to camp before nightfall.

"Guillaume! Radisson! Go fetch two sleds," Godefroy ordered. "And hurry!"

Their work was far from done. Their victory savoured, now they had to run to make sure the moose wasn't devoured during the night by wild animals. Côté, who had already been running for a long time, fell behind Radisson. They looked for the path they had made that morning to save their strength, but drifting snow had almost erased it. The run was tiring, especially the long uphill stretch to the camp. Radisson was surprised to find himself sweating just as much as at the height of summer. He was terribly thirsty and ate snow picked up by his mitt on the way past. Thoughts raced around his head.

Why had Godefroy not offered up part of the moose as a sacrifice? That's what Penikawa had done right after killing the deer. His brother Ganaha, too. The moose was so strong, so beautiful that it had to be thanked for giving up its life to them. And if they weren't going to thank the Indian spirits, then they should thank God. He could feel the immense, rich, and generous nature around him command him to do it and he said a short prayer to himself: "Thank you, God, for giving us this food." But something wasn't quite right. He wasn't sure what.

He took off a mitt and grabbed hold of his knife. A current of energy ripped through him, without him being able to say where it came from, or what it was. He felt as much an Iroquois as a Frenchman. The sensation relieved him a little. He made it up the last of the slope with new enthusiasm. Once at the camp, he took two sleds and trailed them behind him on his way back down. He met Côté, who turned around. Both followed their own trail back to the moose. The sun was disappearing behind the hills by the time they were back beside the moose. Godefroy and Dandonneau had finished gutting it and had cut it in two. The men tied each half onto a sled and set off right away. They were back at the camp by nightfall, almost having to feel their way in the dark, beneath a cloud-covered sky. There was no sign of the Algonquins. But the four

Frenchmen were not worried about them at all. They had brought all they needed with them to spend a day or two in the woods.

One of the Algonquins returned to camp the following morning. They had killed a second moose and it was so heavy they needed help bringing it back. They made the return trip by day's end, just in time to take shelter. The snow was falling more and more heavily now, and the wind had picked up. A storm raged all night long.

In the small hours of the morning, a thick covering of snow had piled up on the roof of animal hide, which was threatening to give way. They took turns all day clearing the roof and freeing the ventilation hole. Otherwise smoke might build up too quickly in the shelter and smother them. The wind made it hard to keep the fire burning and flurries of snow half-extinguished it. It grew colder and colder inside the shelter. The air was stuffy. The men lay on the ground under beaver pelts, coughing slightly, their eyes stinging from the smoke. Radisson could now see the dangers of winter he had been told about. The snow and the cold could prove fatal to the inexperienced. The howling of the wind, zero visibility, and the slaps he got in the face from the snow every time it was his turn to clear the shelter taught him a lesson he would never forget. Time passed slowly. There was nothing to do but hunker down and wait.

The storm wore itself out at the end of the day, but they were not able to head back to Trois-Rivières before gathering all their gear from under the snow and building two new sleds to carry the moose on. The storm had damaged part of the shelter. The last night was the hardest and coldest of all.

Homeward bound, the new sleds did not slide as well over snow that was deeper than ever. The men sank into the snow in places, despite their snowshoes. The dogs had a tough time of it. They took a full day to reach the banks of the Saint-Maurice, instead of the half day it had taken them on the way out. After another day of slow going, even though they put in more effort than ever, Godefroy divided the group in two. Four men and the dogs would bring back the moose and the best sleds to Trois-Rivières, while he and Radisson would stay put with the rest of the gear. They would wait for help in a small shelter they took no time to build.

To pass the time, Radisson hunted hares not far from camp. From time to time, he was happy enough to admire the superb snowscapes the storm had left behind, a whimsical artist that had draped nature with giant ridges and valleys, as though hewn by knife and ironed smooth. The sky and the snow were as pure as prayer. Around the evening fire, they had ample time to go back over the visit from the Iroquois.

"As soon as I saw them go by," Godefroy said, "I wondered where those who had come with them were hiding. Because four people can't make such a long trip in the winter. It's too difficult. I asked the Algonquins to patrol and make sure no one saw them. They found them. There were twelve of them waiting for the emissaries you met. I had them kept under surveillance the whole time, just in case they decided to ambush us and take prisoners, as they tend to do. But they really did come in peace. They stayed very quiet and waited for their chiefs. They didn't even hunt so as not to draw attention to themselves. They had enough provisions with them."

Radisson still didn't really feel like Pierre Godefroy's son. His assurance and authority intimidated him. François' death was also too fresh in the memory. And his desire for Godefroy's daughter wasn't making things any easier... she was a little like his sister. All this stood in his way. What's more, the captain wasn't much of a traveller. He had never visited the Hurons like Ragueneau, Véron (Marguerite's late husband), or Claude Volant. Godefroy had never lived among the Iroquois, like he had. That made a world of difference in Radisson's eyes. The captain did have experience and know-how, but he didn't feel as close to him as he would have liked.

"I'm certain the Iroquois are asking for the Hurons because they want to weaken us," Godefroy went on. "Judging by what Médard Chouart told me—and he worked for the Jesuits among the Hurons for a long time—a few of the Hurons' best warriors took refuge on Île d'Orléans. The Iroquois want to make sure we don't have them, that's for sure."

Radisson didn't really agree. Their intimate surroundings emboldened him. He took a chance and contradicted the captain.

"I think that Andoura, the chief who concluded the negotiations with us, is telling the truth. He really does want to adopt the Hurons as brothers and treat them well."

"What does that change?" Godefroy asked, with the hint of a smile. "Think about it. Any Huron is going to rather be adopted than exterminated, that's for sure. Hundreds have become Iroquois already. But lots of them hate us. They're not happy we ruined their land and they would be pleased to see the back of us if the Iroquois forced us to go back to France or wiped us out completely. But it doesn't matter to us if the Iroquois kill them or adopt them. We're going to lose allies either way. It can only weaken us."

Radisson realized he had misread the situation, but took his idea further.

"The Iroquois are our allies now... "

"Do you really think so? Let me know how that's going in two or three years' time. Médard Chouart and I are the ones who are right, along with all those who support us. We need to keep the Algonquins, Hurons, and all the smaller nations around the Great Lakes on our side, anyone who traded with us in the past. We all need to join forces and get ready to go back to fighting the Iroquois. Because it's going to happen. They'll take up arms against us again, mark my words."

Radisson didn't have an answer. The captain's opinion was based on so many years of experience that he was starting to worry about his trip. Was he doing the right thing risking his life over there?

"Don't worry about going," Godefroy added. "As long as you don't outstay your welcome, you have nothing to fear from the Iroquois. They'll try and get everything they can out of us before switching sides. The Jesuits and the governor say yes to everything they ask for. They're smart enough to make the most of it."

Radisson wanted to meet with the Iroquois again to understand how they had influenced him. He wanted to meet a shaman and question Andoura. He had to go back to their lands. And once there, he would have a clearer idea of their intentions.

"I have something else to tell you. I had the four emissaries followed when they left Trois-Rivières. You remember one of them was seriously ill? Well, he was dead by the time they met with those waiting for them. They held a small ceremony, fastened him to a sled, and brought him back with them. You know it's never good when an emissary dies during a negotiation? The Iroquois see it as a bad sign. I wanted you to know."

Radisson also thought it augured badly. He knew the Iroquois superstitions. The death of a chief favourable to the French could only work against them. It was bad news.

It took four days for the two Algonquins, Côté, and Dandonneau to return with three more men. The group made it back to Trois-Rivières without incident. The frozen moose meat was cut into pieces with an axe and shared equally between the six hunters and the Jesuits. The men who came to help were also given a small share. Even though it was Lent, Ragueneau gave permission to organize a feast for the whole village. It was a great opportunity to treat themselves to a delicious meal.

‖‖‖

CHAPTER 9

ONE STEP BACK, ONE STEP FORWARD

THE GOOD TIMES WERE OVER as quickly as they had begun.

Father Ragueneau was keen to meet with the governor of the colony. The matter at hand was too important to send news of it with a messenger. Accompanied by Radisson, Leboeme, and Pierre Boucher, he travelled from Trois-Rivières to Québec before the spring weather made getting around more difficult.

Radisson loved travelling in winter. He enjoyed the bracing air, the light that shone down on the immaculate snow, the views that stretched as far as the eye could see through the bare forests, the clear tracks left behind by game, the magical way the sleds glided across the frozen surface. The evenings were lively around the campfire and in their makeshift shelters. Winter unveiled another world that was more austere, but more precious, too. It magnified many times over the value of each moment spent in comfort, the value of life itself as it stubbornly shone through the harsh conditions.

They were fortunate enough to be travelling in good weather. Father Ragueneau took control and hurried them along. His unfailing determination and high spirits galvanized their efforts. By making this detour to Québec, Radisson was aware the Jesuit was already preparing his trip to Iroquois country. It was an encouraging sign.

They took only five days to reach the capital.

After spending the night in the Jesuits' college—its grandeur and stone walls reminding Radisson of the cities of France—Ragueneau brought Radisson with him to meet the governor, Jean de Lauson. His residence was at the top of Cap Diamant, a stone's throw from the cliff. The new Jesuit superior, Jean De Quen, accompanied them.

Radisson waited his turn in a sombre room filled with hundreds of books. He had never seen so many! He wondered what use they might be and if it was possible to read so much. In the faint light of the fire that turned the hearth red, he was busy deciphering a few words printed on the leather when Father Ragueneau suddenly opened the door to the governor's office and beckoned him in.

The room was sparsely decorated and had only basic furniture. An eye-catching portrait of a smartly dressed man in a wig—no doubt the king of France, whom the governor represented in the colony—hung from a wall. Sunlight flooded into the room through two large latticed windows overlooking the river. The view was spectacular. Governor Lauson, a short man, was sitting behind a large wooden desk with twisted feet. He looked at Radisson good-naturedly. Radisson wasn't much impressed by the plump old man. The two Jesuits stood on either side of him.

"They tell me you lived a long time with the Iroquois," said Lauson.

"For two years, sir. With the Mohawks."

"And you speak their tongue fluently?"

"I do, sir."

"Very well," the governor acquiesced. "Father Ragueneau is counting on you to assist him when you are with the Onondaga, along with the Hurons they asked from us. We have decided it serves no purpose to oppose this request."

Radisson felt as though the decision was no concern of his. He remarked Father Ragueneau's resigned expression.

"They tell me you are the man who prepared last summer's expedition and that you will prepare this summer's, too. Your master says you have a great talent for this."

"I try my best, sir."

"You should allow sufficient space for some fifty Hurons who are no longer of help to us here. They are a bad influence on our settlers. They were of greater use when they would bring back great quantities of furs. If the Iroquois wish to take some of them off our hands, so much the better. We do want to please them."

Radisson was amazed to hear the governor speak this way. Ragueneau had asked him to argue the case for limiting the extent to which they would honour the promise, by saying he had seen Hurons treated as slaves when he lived among the Mohawks, for example. But judging by the look on Ragueneau's face—every word from the governor dealt him a hammer blow—the matter was no longer up for discussion. Jean de Quen looked calmer. Radisson ventured a comment to help his master.

"I hear some of them are good warriors…"

"We have all the soldiers we need," Lauson responded. "The main thing is to remain at peace with the Iroquois."

"We have invested a great deal in the Iroquois mission," explained Jean de Quen. "The Huron adventure is behind us. Now, we must look forward. A lasting peace with the Iroquois will be of benefit to all the colony."

Radisson wondered why he had been called in. Everything seemed to have been settled.

"Father Ragueneau tells us you are interested in the fur trade. Is that so?"

"Yes, sir."

"One of our objectives is to revive trade by allying with the Iroquois," the governor explained. "I have taken charge personally so that the prosperity of past days might return, but nothing has helped. I therefore ask you to do your utmost to trade with the Iroquois, along with other Frenchmen who will have the same task, for as you know, trade is vital to the colony."

"I will do my best, sir. I promise you that."

"We also ask you to reveal nothing of our conversation to whomsoever," added Jean de Quen. "I remind you that I am your superior and you must do as I say. Everything concerning the decisions made by our governor and our Society must stay between us."

"I will not say a word, Father. You can be sure of it."

"Very well," concluded the governor. "This conversation is over."

Father Ragueneau had found no way to protect the Hurons. Radisson was disappointed.

The heat and the waiting were unbearable. A prisoner to his black soutane and his commitments, Father Ragueneau was becoming more discouraged by the day. He feared seeing his project compromised for good. Because the Iroquois had not respected the agreement. They had not arrived on the longest day of summer as promised.

The makeshift camp the Hurons and the French had made just outside Montréal was becoming more uncomfortable by the day. They had been ready to spend a few days there and now a month had passed. Had something happened to the Iroquois? Had they changed their minds after learning that Mohawks had attacked the Hurons who had sought refuge on Île d'Orléans? Doubt and inactivity were eating away at Ragueneau's morale. Sitting in front of his teepee in the middle of the camp, the Jesuit sweated profusely under the baking July sun.

Radisson would have liked to do more to help him, even though he had already found extra canoes in Montréal, improved the water supply, and bought the food they needed. Much as he would have liked to, he wasn't able to conjure up the Iroquois at the foot of the Lachine rapids! And he couldn't correct the mistake made by the Frenchmen who had allowed the Mohawks to walk off with dozens of Huron prisoners without lifting a finger.

The Hurons with them had explained everything. In May, three hundred Mohawks launched a surprise attack on Île d'Orléans. They killed a number of Hurons and took around sixty of them as prisoners. They brazenly walked past Québec in broad daylight with them, chanting their death song. The French hadn't done a thing to free the Hurons. Radisson had never seen Indians as angry with the French. Of the hundred Hurons on the expedition, most had agreed to go to the Onondaga out of spite, reckoning they had nothing left to lose. They no longer considered themselves to be in an alliance with the French and feared further Mohawk attacks. They hoped the Onondaga would be less cruel. The Hurons who wished to remain in the colony had moved to within a stone's throw of Governor Lauson's residence in Québec. That way the French would have to defend them if the Mohawks attacked again.

The more time passed, the more Radisson was leaning toward the side of Godefroy, Chouart, and all those who refused to turn their backs on the old alliances. Since he had committed himself to following Father Ragueneau, though, he kept his word. Backing out was out of the question, even though the torture he had faced at the hands of the Mohawks would sometimes return to haunt him at night.

Ragueneau wanted to consult the fort commander in Montréal, Monsieur de Maisonneuve, even though the Jesuits were not on very good terms with him. Ragueneau no longer knew what to do: wait a while longer or cancel the expedition. De Maisonneuve was a man of experience, bold but sensible. He had fended off many Iroquois attacks and might have some advice for him. If he gave up and went back to Trois-Rivières, Ragueneau knew the fifty Frenchmen already living among the Onondaga would be in danger. The stakes were high.

When he returned from his visit to Monsieur de Maisonneuve, the Jesuit took Radisson to one side.

"Bring your musket and follow me. We can't be too careful these days."

As the evening advanced, the air grew milder and more comfortable. A welcome breeze picked up, rippling the reflection of the dark blue sky on the surface of the river. Radisson gathered dry wood and lit a small fire to help them see. Father Ragueneau ate a few mouthfuls of bread in silence. He drank some water from the river. Radisson waited patiently until his master was ready to speak.

"You know how much I trust you," Ragueneau said at last. "That's why I will speak openly with you. I need to confide in someone who will not judge me. Of course, I hope you will support me, but I ask you to be frank. Go ahead and contradict me, if you think I am wrong. Because doubt is still eating away at me."

Radisson was flattered, and ready to perform the role Ragueneau expected of him.

"I need your knowledge of the Iroquois to confirm or contradict the decision I have come to. We shall go to the

Onondaga, however risky the expedition. We shall wait here as long as is necessary. That said, I must admit I have serious reserves about what this undertaking has in store for us."

Radisson was of the same opinion.

"Nevertheless, I believe we must go to our compatriots. They are waiting for us and counting on us. We need to bring them what Father Le Moyne asked me for."

"I have put everything together, Father. And then some. We will have everything."

The Jesuit stared into the flames of the small fire that lit their faces. A full moon rose above the river.

"As promised, we shall bring the Hurons who agreed to come with us. I will go through with it, even after what happened on Île d'Orléans, because I see no way of avoiding this sacrifice. Now listen, Radisson. I shall tell you how I really feel, but first promise me you won't repeat a word to anyone."

"I swear, Father."

"You have no doubt remarked that many Hurons no longer trust me. I can tell them I had nothing to do with our governor's decision not to defend them, that I am sorry he did not act. I can remind them of all I did for them when the Iroquois destroyed their land and we sought refuge together in Québec. It doesn't matter what I say. My words blow over their head like the wind. Truth be told, it appears they no longer trust a single Frenchman."

"That's possible," Radisson replied. "They are very angry. They feel betrayed."

"Betrayed is the word. And yet that was not our intention, at least certainly not mine. But now I fear for them. I fear for what will happen to them among the Onondaga. Will they be treated like slaves? I fear they will. Some might even get killed, even though that seems impossible to me when I consider it rationally and I recall the words of Andoura. But I just cannot let go of the thought."

Ragueneau stopped to look at Radisson. He appeared to be overwhelmed.

"I don't know how we're going to get out of this mess, Radisson. I really don't. It is my intention to constantly remind the Iroquois of their commitment to adopt them as brothers. I will stress that. But we will have to keep a close eye on them and hope that the word of the Onondaga is worth more than that of the Mohawks, who have double-crossed us many times now. Tell me frankly: what do you think of all this?"

Radisson was in the same state of mind: he no longer knew which way to turn. But he shared Ragueneau's opinion: better to first respect the agreement between them and move forward from there.

"When I lived with the Mohawks," he said, "I saw just how powerful the advocates for war were. Nothing could change their mind. But there were genuine advocates for peace among them, and I am sure there are more of them among the Onondaga. I think you are right, Father. We must go."

"You have put my mind at ease. So you think there's hope?"

"I think so, yes."

Ragueneau gave a feeble smile.

"We will have to be on our guard at all times," he added. "As soon as the Iroquois arrive—if they ever arrive—mix with them as much as possible. Listen in on their conversations. Observe what they are up to. You know their language and ways. You will be able to see their true intentions easier than I can. We will review the situation together every day."

"Good idea, Father. I'll do that."

Ragueneau opened his mouth to speak, but stopped at the last moment, as though the words he was going to say had burned his tongue.

"Don't let me down," he said at last. "I need you, Radisson. I need your support and your know-how. It's a terrible weight on my mind, you know, moving ahead with such a risky mission. I can see that now."

"It's all going to work out, Father. Together, we'll get there. Don't lose heart."

The Adventures of Radisson, 3
The Incredible Escape will be available in July 2015.

Achevé d'imprimer
sur les presses de
Imprimerie H.L.N.
Imprimé au Canada - Printed in Canada